A smile began to fade as the large, massively muscled, Dr. Eli Clark, came closer.

He'd filled out since she'd last seen him.

He'd never been scrawny, or short, before, but he'd never been this...well...*developed*. But the grin was the same. The eyes, the same.

The boy she'd known as Eli Johns, the boy who'd teased her and played jokes on her endlessly at the orphanage they'd lived in.

That boy who somehow struck lucky and found a family.

Was now Dr. Eli Clark.

Her boss.

Waiting for her with that same cheeky grin across his face, like his next prank was already waiting...

T0014746

Dear Reader,

I'd recently read a book about a family having to settle in the wilds of Alaska and adapting to this new way of life and knew I wanted to set a book there of my own.

But who to place there? What if it was a woman seeking refuge? Someone who thought her anonymity would be guaranteed in such an isolated place, not realizing that the isolation in those places brings the people that are there together?

And then I thought, what if the hero was someone whom she thought she'd never see again? Someone from her past? Someone who knew her? Someone who could get close, when that was the last thing she needed?

And so, Charlie and Eli arrived on the page in the fictional town of Vasquez, which I populated with what I hope are memorable characters, who become patients and newfound family.

I had such fun creating their story. I hope you have as much fun reading it.

Louisa x

Single Mom's Alaskan Adventure

LOUISA HEATON

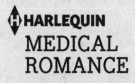

HARLEQUIN
MEDICAL
ROMANCE

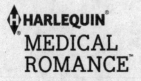

HARLEQUIN®
MEDICAL
ROMANCE™

Recycling programs
for this product may
not exist in your area.

ISBN-13: 978-1-335-59539-3

Single Mom's Alaskan Adventure

Copyright © 2024 by Louisa Heaton

Harlequin Enterprises ULC
22 Adelaide St. West, 41st Floor
Toronto, Ontario M5H 4E3, Canada
www.Harlequin.com

Printed in U.S.A.

Louisa Heaton lives on Hayling Island, Hampshire, with her husband, four children and a small zoo. She has worked in various roles in the health industry—most recently four years as a community first responder, answering emergency calls. When not writing, Louisa enjoys other creative pursuits, including reading, quilting and patchwork—usually instead of the things she *ought* to be doing!

Books by Louisa Heaton

Harlequin Medical Romance

Yorkshire Village Vets

Bound by Their Pregnancy Surprise

Greenbeck Village GPs

The Brooding Doc and the Single Mom
Second Chance for the Village Nurse

Night Shift in Barcelona

Their Marriage Worth Fighting For

A GP Worth Staying For
Their Marriage Meant To Be
A Date with Her Best Friend
Miracle Twins for the Midwife
Snowed In with the Children's Doctor

Visit the Author Profile page
at Harlequin.com for more titles.

For Lorna and Bonny x

CHAPTER ONE

CHARLIE GRIFFIN HAD been told she would need to make two flights to get to the remote town of Vasquez, Alaska, and had assumed, as anyone would, that this would mean two proper aeroplanes.

How wrong could I be?

The first flight had been easy enough, and her daughter, Alice, had sat and watched a cartoon movie for most of it, holding her teddy, and Charlie knew that they would be met and escorted to their second plane, which would bring them into Vasquez. She figured it would be a kind of meet-and-greet service that would whisk her through all the security checks and baggage reclaim and, to a point, it was. But the guy in cargo shorts and a sign that had her name on it led her away from the airport and out towards a car.

Charlie stopped, holding her daughter's hand. 'There's meant to be a second flight that takes us to Vasquez. Have you got the right Griffin?'

The guy, who'd introduced himself as Chuck,

grinned, chewing gum, and nodded. 'That's right. Your next plane is in the bay.'

'The *bay*?'

'It's a seaplane. Ain't no airport in Vasquez… you come in and land on the water.'

'Oh.' Suddenly she wasn't sure. But wasn't this what she wanted? Somewhere remote? Vasquez, Alaska, fitted that bill perfectly. The perfect hide-away for her and Alice. To go someplace where nobody would know her. She preferred to hide. To keep mobile and have no one know her shame and, most importantly of all, *never* become the next hot topic of conversation.

'I get it. I'm a strange guy. Look…' Chuck pulled a piece of paper from his pocket and handed it to her. 'That's the number of the clinic you'll be working at. Why don't you give them a ring and they'll confirm what I'm saying? So you know you're not just getting in a vehicle with someone you shouldn't.' Chuck went and sat in the car.

She had to be cautious. She'd learned that a lot lately. There was paperwork in her purse with the clinic's number on, too. She pulled it out and checked the number against the one Chuck had given her. It was the same. But she wouldn't take any chances. So she phoned the number, told them who she was and the receptionist confirmed that Chuck was who he said he was and that she was perfectly safe to get into his car.

The engine was idling by the time she opened the back door and got in with Alice. 'Buckle up, baby,' she said, reaching over Alice to strap her in. 'How far to the bay?'

'Twenty minutes, if traffic's okay.'

'Thank you.'

'No problem.' Chuck smiled at her in the rear-view mirror and drove them away from the airport. As the journey continued she pulled her instructions and second ticket from her purse and now understood why it looked different from the first. The instructions had said she'd be met after her first flight and escorted to the second, but they could at least have mentioned it was a car ride away.

When they pulled up alongside a big stretch of water, Alice gaped out of the window. 'Is that our plane?'

Charlie hoped not. It didn't look fit to fly! It had to be at least thirty or more years old. It looked battered. Ancient. And was that *rust* she could see? Dirt? She hoped it was dirt. 'I don't know. Chuck, is that…?'

'Sure is! Best seaplane on the Alaskan coast.'

The best? 'What does the worst look like?' she muttered under her breath, trying to put a brave face on things as she dragged her cases out of the trunk of the car.

Alice was excited. She'd never even flown before today. Now she'd experienced a jet and a raggedy old seaplane… This was all an adventure to her and Charlie wished she had the same optimism as her daughter.

Adjusting her sunglasses onto the top of her head to hold back her long hair, she dragged the cases along the pier. The wheels bumped and jolted the cases all over the place and, once or twice, Charlie thought she might lose them in the bay, which looked dark and forbidding. Her heels kept slipping into the gaps too, tripping her, and she must have looked quite ungainly.

Chuck opened the doors and loaded the cases into the back and then helped Alice, then Charlie up into the plane. 'Seat belts on, ladies.' And then he climbed through to the cockpit.

'Wait, you're our pilot, too?'

'You bet!' Chuck grinned, gave them a thumbs up and then reached for a large set of headphones, which he placed on his head, and then began flicking switches and starting up the engine.

It choked a couple of times before the engine started and Charlie began to wish that she had some sort of faith she could cling to. In the meantime, she simply smiled at her daughter, who seemed to be incredibly excited at this new adventure, and hoped that this old rust bucket would get them to Vasquez safely.

'How long?' she called to Chuck.

'Little over an hour,' he called back as the plane began to move away from the short pier.

An hour. She could do an hour, right?

Lift-off was bumpier than she expected, but Alice loved it. 'Yee-haw!' she cried out as they hit another small wave before the seaplane made it into the air.

Just get us there in one piece, Chuck.

Charlie gripped the edge of her seat and wished she'd had the foresight to include travel sickness tablets in her hand luggage. She'd never needed them before, but this small seaplane seemed to feel and experience every piece of turbulence that existed in the air and it dipped and bumped and rattled loudly with every disturbance.

'What made ya want to come to Vasquez? It's a little out of the way for city folks like you,' asked Chuck, looking over his shoulder.

'Oh, you know…needed a change of pace,' she said, teeth chattering.

Chuck laughed. 'You'll get that! It's a different way of life out there, you know? Probably nothing like you're used to.'

'Great.'

That's just what I need.

'You got the Internet out there in Vasquez?'

'Oh, yeah. All the mod cons. It ain't reliable, though. Thing goes on the fritz more often than not, so most folks have a CB radio on hand, just in case they need to call for help.'

Citizens Band radios. Wow. Charlie had thought those things were obsolete. But it made sense if you lived in the middle of nowhere, which was exactly where Vasquez was. And an unreliable Internet sounded perfect.

'What do you do in Vasquez, Chuck?'

'I mush.'

Charlie blinked. She must have heard wrong. 'I'm sorry, what?'

'I mush dogs. Train them for racing. You know, for dog sledding? I raise huskies, breed them, work them when the tourists come a calling.'

'You have dogs?' asked Alice, suddenly enraptured. Alice loved animals more than anything and had been persuaded that Vasquez would be an amazing place for her to indulge her fascination with wildlife.

'Forty-two of them and counting.'

'Mom! He's got forty-two dogs!'

'I heard, honey. Do you need that many, Chuck? I mean…how many tourists do you get?'

Chuck laughed. 'Most of those are pups. I'm just waiting for them to be old enough to go to their new homes. Racers and the like. I got champions in my line and they fetch a pretty price. But when they're gone, I'll only have like sixteen.'

Only sixteen dogs.

Charlie smiled, unable to imagine it. 'What can you tell me about the people?'

'Oh, they're a friendly bunch. Most people live in town, but there are a few homesteads that are isolated, so you don't get to see those folks as often.'

'And Dr Clark? What's he like?' Dr Clark was going to be her boss. He'd emailed her once or twice to let her know her responsibilities during her temporary contract covering for some doctor that had gone on maternity leave. His emails had been short. Sweet.

'Eli? Oh, he's great. Best doctor we've ever had.'

Eli. She'd known an Eli once and it hadn't been the greatest of experiences. But that was a long time ago, in a different life. She didn't have to worry about that any more. It was in the past and she'd moved on. Just as he had, most probably.

'I've had to fly him out to patients in the past, if we couldn't get there by car or dog sled.'

'You don't have ambulances?'

'I am the ambulance.' He laughed and turned back around.

Charlie raised her eyebrows.

I wanted remote. I'm getting remote.

Alice was open-mouthed as she gazed out of the windows of the small seaplane. They flew over some gorgeous country—snow-capped mountains, glaciers, lakes, hills of green, the occasional small town. But mostly Charlie could feel the immensity of the space they were in. The city and all its hectic complications, its computers and endless streams of invasive social media were far behind her and with every mile that passed she felt some of her stress ebbing away with it. There was something soothing about looking out at all that country. At the peace of it. The anonymity of it. Its vastness made all her worries seem insignificant. And the sky… The sky was never-ending. An eternity of blue and space. She dared hope that she could lose herself beneath it and somehow be reborn into the woman she used to be. The Charlie she'd been before meeting Glen.

'Mom, I think I can see a bear!' Alice pointed down at a brown speck that seemed to be making its way alongside a river.

Maybe it was a bear. Maybe it was a moose? Or an elk? It was hard to say. 'I can see it, baby.'

'You like bears?' asked Chuck.

'I do! They're my favourite animal in the whole wide world!' enthused Alice, squeezing her own teddy tightly.

'Well, plenty of grizzlies near Vasquez. You keep your distance. Especially from the mama bears, you hear? They're not as sweet and nice as the one you've got there.'

'I will.'

Charlie felt slightly alarmed by this piece of news, but also protective. She was her own mama bear and would do anything to protect her child from danger. 'How much further?' she asked Chuck.

'You see that lake down there to your right? With the settlement alongside it?'

'I do.'

'That's Vasquez. That's home.'

They both gazed down upon it. Vasquez seemed to have been built on a headland that jutted out from the eastern side of the lake. To the west were snow-capped mountains, but Vasquez and the land around it were verdant and green. There was a forest and within it a river that seemed to feed into the lake and, beyond the river, hills and rocks and the occasional homestead.

'Better be ready. Landings can be bumpy.'

Charlie checked Alice's belt first, then redid her own lap belt, fussing with it until it felt right and having one last moment where she hoped she was doing the right thing for both of them.

The plane banked as Chuck turned it to approach Vasquez from the south and then he slowly began to descend. The green became more defined as plants and trees and grass, the buildings along the waterfront became more apparent—a B & B, a diner, a groceries store. And they all seemed to belong to the Clarks—Clark's Diner. Clark's B & B. Clark's General Store. And before she could think about that some more, the plane hit the water, bouncing slightly until it aquaplaned smoothly for a while, the engine dying down as the battered old bucket of a vehicle delivered them safely to another wooden pier.

Chuck got out first, mooring the plane with ropes, and then helped Alice out first, offering a steadying hand to Charlie as she disembarked. 'Boss is here,' he said, grinning and indicating behind her, with a brief nod of his head and a salute to the unseen man behind them.

Dr Clark had said he'd meet them so he could drive them straight to their residence—a two-bedroomed property owned by Dr Clark's own mother. From what Charlie understood, the Clarks owned a lot of property and businesses in Vasquez.

She wanted to make a great first impression, even though she was here only temporarily to cover a maternity contract, and so she adjusted her sunglasses onto the top of her head again, straightened and turned around, with a smile upon her face. A smile that began to fade as the large, massively muscled Dr Eli Clark came closer.

He'd filled out since she'd last seen him.

He'd never been scrawny or short before, but he'd never been this...well...*developed*. But the grin was the same. The eyes, the same.

The boy she'd known as Eli Johns, the boy who'd teased her and played jokes on her endlessly at the orphanage they'd lived in.

That boy who had somehow struck lucky and found a family.

Was now Dr Eli Clark.

Her boss.

Waiting for her with that same cheeky grin across his face, as if his next prank was already waiting…

CHAPTER TWO

'Eli?'

There was so much he wanted to say. So much he could say, but, rather than answer her straight away, he knelt so he could be on the same level as her daughter. 'Hey there. What's your name?'

The daughter was the spitting image of her mother. Long, dark brown hair, same dark brown eyes. Like melted chocolate. The same bone structure.

'Alice.'

She seemed shy, but she was smiling and she had a beautiful smile, too. 'Hey, Alice. Who's that?' he asked, pointing to the teddy bear that she carried with her.

'Mr Cuddles.'

'Mr Cuddles?' He glanced up at Charlie and registered the shock that was still painted large across her face. 'Well, he sounds like a very friendly bear. Can I shake his paw?'

Alice giggled slightly and held out the bear.

Eli gently took a paw and shook it. 'Nice to

meet you, Mr Cuddles. I'm Eli. Is it okay if I talk to your mom for a little while now?'

Alice nodded.

He stood, towering over Charlie and her little girl. He'd always been slightly taller than Charlie, but he'd clearly not finished growing before he got adopted and now he was a good head and a half taller than she. 'I hoped it was you, when I saw your name.'

'Really? You *hoped*? I've emailed you six times since accepting this posting—you didn't think to tell me who you really were?'

He grinned. 'I thought it could be a surprise.'

'Oh, it's definitely that,' she replied, not sounding the least bit happy about it and looking at anything that wasn't his face.

He got it. When they'd been kids, she'd often told him that she could have quite happily punched him in the nose every time he had grinned at her, and he couldn't help but grin now. He liked that they were being reunited. Here was someone who understood his past better than anyone else in Vasquez. And she was only here a short time. It was why he'd agreed to hire her.

'You don't seem thrilled.'

'Why would I be?' Now she looked at him. Intently so and he realised as he stared back that she'd changed too. As a young teen, she'd been scrawny and much too thin. But now, as a grown woman, she'd developed. He noted the hint of delicious curves beneath her blouse and skirt and those heels she was wearing? Well, he couldn't remember the last time he saw a woman wearing heels in Vasquez. Most people wore boots of some kind.

The heels drew his eye to parts of her anatomy that he really ought not to stare at. Little Charlie Griffin had grown from a gauche, skinny teen with angry acne into a beautiful, elegant young woman. A mother herself! And though he wondered what the story was there and why she was alone and hadn't brought a partner, he knew he would not ask. Not yet, anyway. Time would reveal all. It always did. But he envied her the fact that she had real family. That blood connection. The Clarks might have taken him in, made him one of their own, given him their name and their love, but they weren't blood. Eli had always hoped that one day he would have a family of his own. Get married, have loads of kids, but even that had been taken away from him.

So yeah. He envied her having achieved something he never would.

'Aren't reunions meant to be happy occasions?' He grinned, holding out his arms as if suggesting she ought to step into them and give him a hug.

She smiled back. A fake smile. One that didn't touch her eyes. 'You'd think so.' And she side-stepped him, pulling her cases behind her, not realising that the pier was not as wide as she hoped.

The case rumbled over the edge and, before she knew it, the weight of it caused it to slip from her fingers as it caught on the slats and tumbled with a big splash into the water.

'No!' she yelled, collapsing to her knees to try and grab for it as it floated near her, her arms not long enough to grasp it.

Eli tried his hardest not to smile, but he couldn't help it. It was kind of funny. If she'd not been in such a snoot with him, it wouldn't have happened at all. 'Want some help?'

'I don't need any help from you, thank you very much!' she snarled.

'Okay.' He stood there, arms crossed, watching her as she tried to reach her case to no avail. She stretched and grunted and even, at one point, got up to grab a thin stick from the shore to try and prod the case back towards her. Unfortunately she only succeeded in pushing her case further away from her and it began to float away into the bay.

'Damn it!'

'Mom, you swore.'

Charlie turned to look at her daughter. 'Sorry, baby.' But then she glanced up at him. Those chocolate eyes of hers angry and furious.

He knew she would not ask him again, but he also knew he couldn't leave her stranded like this, with the majority of her possessions that she'd brought with her floating away into the bay. Eli began to undo his boots.

'What are you doing?' she asked.

'Helping out.' He pulled off the boots and then his socks. He knew the water would be cold. It always was here in Vasquez, even when they had warmer days and the sun shone, as it did today. The water could be deceptive. Eli didn't bother rolling up his jeans. They were going to get wet no matter what he did and so he splashed down into the water and by the time he reached her case? It was up to his waist.

Charlie could not believe her eyes.

Eli was wading through the water to retrieve her case and by the time he got it the water was creeping up his shirt.

She couldn't think about how kind a gesture it was. She was too busy trying to stop thinking about how hot he looked doing so.

Eli was a huge man. Muscled. And…oh, yes… she could see the dark shapes of some sort of tribal tattoo on his arms and back. And with his shaggy locks and beard, the scar through his eyebrow and all of the things that made Eli *Eli*, he looked like a barbarian. The kind of barbarian that you wouldn't mind invading your village and throwing you over his shoulder.

He hefted her heavy case easily, lifting it out of the water, and began the slow wade back to shore.

His jeans were now moulded to his muscled thighs as he emerged from the water like a demigod and set her case down on the ground. He was breathing steadily and she noticed a necklace around his neck, tied with a leather loop. It looked to be a piece of turquoise and it rested on his slightly hairy chest, drawing her eye. Lust smacked into her like a tsunami.

'Thank you,' she managed.

'No problem.' He smiled at her, as if knowing the effect he was having on her, and for that she didn't like him even more. Felt her anger grow again as she watched him pull his socks onto his wet feet, and then his boots.

'I know you said you'd take us to where we're staying, but if you just give me the address, I'm sure we can find it on our own. You're soaked...' Her gaze drifted over his body once again. His broad chest. His flat, narrow waist. His toned and shapely thigh muscles. She felt heat surge into her cheeks. 'And you probably want to get changed.'

She did not want to feel this way about Eli! She'd been glad when he'd been adopted. It had meant she didn't have to put up with him any more! But this? This was too much.

'It's just water. My truck's seen worse. Come on.' He stepped ahead of her, leading her towards a flatbed truck that was parked on the side of the road near Clark's Diner.

Not knowing how else she could get out of being in his truck with him, she managed a smile at her daughter and took her hand, following him up the slight incline towards the vehicle.

If it were her, she would have wanted to be out of those wet jeans as soon as possible. She hated the feeling of wet material against her legs. She'd been caught in a sudden downpour once and been soaked. She'd not been able to get into work quick enough to put on some nice dry scrubs and feel comfortable again.

Yet he was still happy to show her around? To sit in those wet jeans? Drive in them? The man was crazy, but then she knew that. He always had been the type to look out for odd things. Strange things. To experience life. Perhaps this meant nothing to him?

Eli hefted her case into the back of his truck and then opened the passenger-side door for her and Alice. 'My ladies.'

Alice giggled and clambered in, so that she would be sitting between them, which suited Charlie just fine. She didn't need to be squashed up against him, feeling his body and his heat against her own.

'Let's get you strapped in.' Eli leaned over her daughter, reaching for her seat belt, his face coming alarmingly close to Charlie's, so that she had to turn away for her own seat belt and stare out of the window, while she blindly tried to click it into position, her hands trembling.

Why were they trembling? Was this just shock

at seeing Eli again? Or was it more to do with her body's alarming response to him? If someone had sat her down and told her that whenever the day occurred that she would meet up with Eli Johns again, she would be sexually attracted to him immediately, Charlie would have laughed with obscene amounts of hilarity in their face. Because nothing of the sort could ever be possible.

And yet here she was.

The engine rumbled into life. 'We all ready?'

She managed a smile and tried not to focus on his large, square hands on the steering wheel. He had lots of thin leather bracelets on his wrists. They were old and worn, but contrasted beautifully with his darker skin tone. Her gaze travelled up his arms, hidden by the flowing shirt he wore, and she couldn't help but wonder what his forearms would look like. She liked forearms. Found them sexy. She didn't know why.

'My mom's been in and spruced up the cottage for you. Fresh bed sheets, some flowers. She's even put some things in your fridge.'

My mom.

Eli had received the most amazing present any kid in an orphanage could receive—adoption. They'd both given up on the idea. Teenagers didn't often get picked by families looking to foster or adopt. They'd been told that they were the hardest to place and it was something that you just learned to accept, and yet Eli had got the best gift in the world. Charlie remembered them coming to the orphanage. Had been aware of them sitting at the back of the room, talking quietly with some of the staff. Then they'd been mucking around with an indoor archery kit and Eli had hit the gold every single time he took a shot. She'd thought he was showing off and he'd gone over to talk to Jason, one of the care workers, who'd been standing with the Clarks, and they'd all begun to laugh and joke with one another and after that day Eli had kept getting invited out for day trips, or weekends with this family and then suddenly Eli was gone. For ever.

Charlie had never wanted to be jealous of Eli ever! But she had been back then. And she'd hated herself for it. She'd tried to make herself feel better by telling herself that at least Eli was gone now and she wouldn't have to put up with his teasing any more, or his practical jokes or the way he'd keep looking at her across the room, as if he was planning his next trick. She'd spent most of her childhood being aware of where he was, just so she could keep an eye out and, with him gone, she didn't have to worry about that any more.

What she hadn't expected to feel after he'd left was how much she'd actually *missed* him. It had hit her, unexpectedly, left her feeling emotionally winded. She'd not realised just how much he'd been a part of her life. The two of them, the oldest ones, watching the younger kids arrive and then going, never to be seen again. Losing Eli had been incredibly difficult to accept. That had been quite the shocker. But time had passed. More kids had arrived. Some others had left. And then Charlie had been accepted into medical school and she'd moved out. Moved away. Begun to live on her own and make her own way in life. And Eli had been mostly forgotten.

Until now.

She had a brief, blurry memory of Mrs Clark. Back then, she'd been a tall woman, dark-haired. Quite pretty. And she'd thought nothing of squatting down to talk to and enjoy the company of some of the younger kids. Charlie had never spoken to her, though. She'd always held back to protect herself. If you didn't have hope, then you couldn't be disappointed.

'You must thank her for me.'

'No doubt you'll run into her at some point. Alice? Are you going to go to the school here in Vasquez?'

Alice looked up at her, uncertainly.

So Charlie answered for her. 'Yes. The one on Pelican Point, I think it's called.'

'Yep. That's the one Mom teaches at. She's probably going to be Alice's teacher.'

'Oh. Right.'

There was a brief uncomfortable silence where she determinedly looked out of the truck window, rather than at him, to observe the passing scenery. Vasquez was a small town. Neat, clean streets. Well-tended, older properties with great gardens. Often, people would notice the truck and give them a wave, smiling broadly, and she realised that Eli was liked here. Loved. Clearly he'd settled well into this place and she was surprised. When she'd known him as a young boy, he'd been into rap music and video games and technology. He'd loved living in the city and she would never have guessed that he would settle so well into a place that was a little more remote. Briefly, she wondered where he'd trained to become a doctor.

Beyond the streets she saw mountains, lush and green at the moment, but the tops of them were obscured by the white clouds that drifted high above. Birds soared high above in the sky, but she didn't know what kind. They looked quite large. Seabirds? Or hunting birds like ospreys or kites?

Maybe she'd learn all of that after being here a few months, and thank goodness there was an end date to her contract and she'd not moved here permanently! Because she really didn't think she'd be able to deal with working with Eli for much longer than she had to.

'Here we go.' Eli hit a left and pulled up at a small log-cabin-style cottage that had some hanging baskets full of flowers either side of the front door. It had a wrap-around porch, with a bench and what looked like a hammock and some potted plants too. 'Home, sweet home.'

'For a little while, anyway.' She felt the need to say it. To remind him that she wasn't here very long. It was what she was used to. Always moving. Never quite settling anywhere. It was why she'd never bought a house. Why she'd never bought a car. Why she always worked as a locum, or covered temporary contracts. It made her feel better to keep on moving. To get to know people for a little while and then move on. Because the past could creep up on you unexpectedly and the internet had a long memory. Something you thought was gone could return in a nanosecond, if people wanted it to.

Eli was already hefting her case out of the back of the truck and pulling it towards the front porch and squatting to the welcome mat, lifting it and retrieving a key.

Quaint.

But she didn't want him in their home. She didn't want to see him in there, all damp and muscly and devastatingly handsome. She wanted him gone, so that she and Alice could look around themselves. Get settled in. She'd have to see Eli at work and that would be enough as it was.

He was already unlocking the door and swinging it open, stepping back so they could pass him.

Alice ran in excitedly, but Charlie paused and took the key from his fingers, trying not to register what it felt like when her fingers brushed his. Like electricity. 'We can get settled in, thanks. I'll see you at the clinic on Monday morning?'

He got the message. Well, she hoped so, when he grinned and folded his arms, leaning against the doorjamb.

'Yes, you will. Eight o'clock sharp. You ready for a taste of Alaskan medicine? It might not be what you're used to.'

She had no idea what he meant. Surely all medicine was the same? 'Of course.'

'Great. Okay. I'll be seeing you,' he said, staring at her and smiling in that ridiculous way he'd had when they were kids. As if he'd got something up his sleeve that she simply wasn't prepared for.

'You will.'

'Mom! Come see the back yard!'

'Excuse me.' And she closed the door on him with some satisfaction.

Eli could wait.

Eli could go home.

And she was going to get settled in and hope that the next few months would fly by.

CHAPTER THREE

THE VASQUEZ MEDICAL CLINIC AND HOSPITAL appeared to be the largest building she'd seen here yet. It was long and low, all on the same storey, but stretched out, abutting the lush green mountain that sat behind it.

Charlie was very nervous of going in. She knew she needn't be. She was a very capable doctor and she was so used to having first days at work. Getting to know everyone, finding out where everything was. One of her strongest skills was adaptation and she prided herself on settling somewhere quickly and easily, to make her working life run smoothly. All she had to do was be friends with these people. They didn't have to have any heart-to-hearts. They never needed to know her past. They just needed her to fit in and do her job and that worked for her.

But here? That was going to be a different story.

Earlier this morning, she'd dropped Alice off at the school. It was her first year in kindergarten, but Charlie had no worries about her daughter fitting in either. Alice was a confident and independent young lady, just as Charlie had taught her to be.

Who is the only person you can rely on?
Me!
Who is the only person who can make you happy?
Me!

Sentences she'd drilled into her from an early age. It was important that Alice understand that the world was a harsh place. Because it was. In the early years, of course, Alice hadn't really known they were moving so much. Last year, in pre-kindergarten, she'd kind of got a little upset at leaving her friends behind, but Charlie knew she would make new ones! And everyone always wanted to be friends with the new kid and Mrs Clark, Eli's adopted mother and Alice's new teacher, had seemed wonderful.

'Charlie! Alice! It's a pleasure to meet you, at last!' Mrs Clark had crouched to smile at Charlie's daughter and shake her hand. 'Eli's told me so much about you, already!'

Had he? What was there to tell? What did *he* even know about her?

'Are you excited, Alice? First day!'

Alice was excited. Of course she was. Charlie had raised a confident daughter, there would be no tears, no clinging to her mother's leg.

'We're going to do lots of fun things today, so I hope you're ready?'

'I'm ready!' Alice took Mrs Clark's hand.

Eli's mother stood again and looked at Charlie. 'Settled in all right? Is everything okay with the cottage?'

'It's great, thank you. And thanks again for putting some foodstuffs in the fridge for us. You didn't have to do that. You must let me know what I owe you.'

'You don't owe me anything! It's an absolute pleasure.'

'No, I insist.'

'Look, I tell you what…you can pay me back by coming over tonight and I'll cook you both a nice hot meal. I'd love for us to sit and chat and get to know one another. Six o clock be okay? My grandkids will be there, so people for Alice to play with.'

Charlie couldn't think of how to get out of it. What to say, so as not to offend this woman? 'It won't seem right you feeding us again, when we're the ones that owe you.'

'Then let's call it a potluck! You make something and bring it over—how does that sound?'

'Er…great. Sure. Thanks.' Charlie smiled, figuring she'd do this the once and then gently extract herself and Alice from Mrs Clark's home, claiming a school night. That she'd need to get

Alice in the bath and then bed before school the next day.

It wasn't that she didn't like Mrs Clark. Far from it. She seemed a lovely, warm and welcoming woman. Her hair a little greyer than before, but still the same genuine smile. But this much attention made Charlie feel uncomfortable. Generally she was introverted and liked her own company. Being with someone so…open and full of life was a little…disturbing. It made her want to retreat and hide so she could breathe again.

She'd glanced at her watch and said goodbye and now she was standing outside the clinic, wondering just what awaited her inside. Had Eli told everyone in there who she was and where she was from? She hoped not, because that wasn't something she told anyone, ever. Her private life was her own and no one needed to know it. Exposure, she'd learned, came at a cost.

Mrs Clark had already superimposed herself into Charlie's life with her expectations, what would Eli do?

She pushed open the glass door and headed inside, her gaze instantly taking in all the information. A reception desk straight ahead. An empty waiting area to her right. This looked like the primary care area of the clinic. There was a corridor in the middle signposting X-Ray, Ultrasound, Day Surgery and Inpatient Care. It was bright. Welcoming. A nurse walked up the corridor in pale green scrubs, before turning into a doorway and disappearing.

Charlie walked up to Reception. Behind it sat a lady who looked to be in her fifties. She was working on a sudoku puzzle. 'Hello. I'm Dr Charlotte Griffin. Dr Clark is expecting me?'

The woman looked up in surprise. 'Oh! Are you the new doctor taking over for Nance? My name's Dorothea. Welcome, we spoke on the phone the other day!'

Charlie smiled. 'Thanks. I can't help but notice that you don't have anyone waiting…is that normal? Or haven't you opened yet?'

'Oh, this is normal! The folks around here are quite hardy. We have to be. We don't go running to our doctor with every little twinge or headache like they do in the big city. It has to be gushing blood or about to fall off before anyone will walk in here!' Dorothea laughed. 'Except for Stewie. You'll meet him soon, no doubt.' She leaned in. 'Bit of health anxiety and keeps us on our toes with all his imagined diagnoses, which we have to check out, just in case.'

'I'll look forward to meeting him.' Charlie was used to frequent fliers. 'And where would I find Dr Clark?'

Dorothea checked her watch. 'He'll be in his office. See that corridor? Down to the end, last door on the right.'

'Thanks. Very nice to meet you, Dorothea.'

'Call me Dot.'

Dot. Okay. Charlie smiled her thanks and began to walk down the corridor, feeling the butterflies in her stomach begin their dance. Sweat began to bloom in her armpits and the small of her back, despite the antiperspirant she'd sprayed on this morning, anticipating such a thing.

It really was ridiculous. She shouldn't be feeling this way.

What I need to do is pretend that I don't know him at all. It's just a normal first day and I want to get stuck into treating patients. Just do the job I'm here to do. Easy, right?

She squared her shoulders and sucked in a breath as she reached his office. His door was open and as she turned the corner to enter, hand raised to rap her knuckles on the door, she expected she'd see him behind his desk, either on the phone, or at his computer completing a report or something.

What she *did not* expect was to see him doing press-ups, bare-chested, down on the ground.

She'd never goggled in her life, but she did in that moment.

He was a thing of beauty. As if he'd been carved. Each muscle apparent across his back and shoulders, his long hair loose, the waves touching the carpet each time he lowered himself down. He had a tattoo in the centre of his upper back, just beneath his neck, of the caduceus. The staff, entwined with two snakes, used to symbolise medics.

She had to lick her lips before she could speak. 'Good morning.'

He grunted one last time as he pushed himself to his feet and turned to face her, his cheeks red with effort, his smile broad. 'Good morning, Dr Griffin! Sorry about this, I usually like to start my day with some cardio exercises.'

Charlie could think of other cardio exercises that might be more fun, but she quickly pushed those thoughts to one side.

Be professional. First day, remember. Pretend you don't know him.

'So do I. It's called getting Alice up and ready for school.'

He smiled that charming and effortlessly cheeky smile of his that made her heart go thumpety-thump, raising her blood pressure by a few points. Which made her feel angry and raised it a little more.

Eli grabbed a towel off his chair and began to wipe himself down with it, before grabbing a loose shirt and shrugging that on, once he'd sprayed himself with some cologne he didn't need. It was unfair enough that he looked as fine as he did, did he really need to smell nice, too?

She turned away as he buttoned his shirt. She wasn't sure why. She'd just seen him half naked, why should she turn away as he put clothes *on*?

But then she figured that getting dressed and undressed was something a person normally did in private and perhaps she didn't want to witness him doing private things? Or maybe it was because she would focus too much on the disappearing sight of his chest and stomach? Either way it was because of lust or etiquette.

Quite frankly Charlie was amazed that his primary care clinic wasn't filled every day with every young woman in town with drooling issues, just so they could spend time with him, being dazzled by his eyes and attention. Imagine what it would feel like to be besotted with Eli and have him sitting close to you as he listened to your chest with his stethoscope... Where would you look exactly? At those eyes? His luscious hair? The shape of his fine arms? Or would you just be so busy trying to slow and calm your breathing?

'Take a seat. Can I get you anything? Coffee? Tea? Juice?' Eli walked to the other side of his desk and got settled in.

'I'm fine, thanks.'

'Okay. Well, I thought for this first week you could shadow me in both the clinic and the hospital and, that way, you'll get to know where everything is and how we work here. I took the courtesy of making your ID card. Here you go.' He pulled a lanyard from his top desk drawer. 'This will log you into the system each time you need it. Just swipe it in the card reader.'

'Great.' She hung it around her neck.

'You'll be expected to take care of patients in the primary care setting, as well as out in the field. We occasionally do house visits. We often get called to accidents themselves.'

'Chuck told me.'

'Yeah. Great guy. He ever tell you about the time we almost had to amputate his leg?'

'No. He didn't.'

'He'll probably save that story for when you're eating. Right! Shall I show you around the place?'

She stood and nodded. 'Sounds perfect.'

She had her walls up. He sensed that immediately. Charlie was trying to show him that she was there to be professional and do the work, but he wished that she'd chill out a little. It was hard trying to be friendly when all the other person would do was give you a tight smile, or a nod.

She'd loosen up, no doubt. She'd have no choice living out here in Vasquez. This wasn't the city. She wasn't living in a place where everyone was strangers. Everyone knew each other here. The same families had lived here for decades. You couldn't walk down the street without stopping to say hello a lot, or passing the time over a garden fence, or waving at someone across the street walking their dog. Everyone relied upon each other here. There was no other way to be when you lived in such an isolated spot.

If you didn't have each other's back, then you wouldn't survive. Alaska could kill you. Easily. There were creatures here that would happily rip you to shreds. The weather could turn in an instant and give you hypothermia, or block off roads, and if you tried to stay within your own bubble here? You wouldn't survive.

She'd begin to understand this at some point, he had no doubt, and he was looking forward to watching her learn. He could tell her outright, but where would the fun in that be? He'd keep an eye on her. Make sure that she and Alice remained safe. He just wouldn't tell her, because he figured that she wouldn't be too happy about that if he got all knight in shining armour on her. But he'd keep an eye out. Help when he was needed. It was always the same with these city folks that came to town. They thought they could continue to live their lives the way they did in the urban jungle, but you just couldn't do that out here. It was a culture shock, that was for sure. Things might be fine right now, but that was because the weather was okay right now, but when it turned?

'I'll show you the primary care clinic first. That's where you'll do the majority of your work.'

'Where do you do the majority of yours?'

'The clinic, but I also do surgeries in the theatre.'

'Impressive.'

'You have to be able to multitask out here.

Some patients wouldn't last if they had to wait for a medical evacuation flight out to a big hospital, so I do what I can here to keep them alive before the big guns arrive.'

'Like a first responder?'

'Pretty much, but you'd be surprised at how much more we do.'

'What was your last big case that got transported out?'

He thought for a moment. 'Cindy Kramer. Pregnant with triplets, naturally. We were all set up, knew how we'd handle it if she made it to term, but she went into labour prematurely at twenty-eight weeks and we simply didn't have the capacity to care for three premature babies of that gestation. Thirty weeks onwards, maybe, but her babies were guesstimated at less than a pound each, it would have been arrogant of us to assume we could help them the best, so we arranged for transport. Before that, it was Ken Palmer. Creutzfeldt-Jakob disease. Cruel way to go. We thought stroke initially. Something neuro definitely, maybe encephalitis or meningitis, and he was deteriorating fast. He got flown to Anchorage and they diagnosed the CJD. He died within the week.'

'It attacks fast.'

Eli nodded. 'Just two weeks prior he'd been telling me about how he'd booked flights to go and visit his grandbabies. He'd been so excited.

Hadn't seen them for three months, not since they were born.' He shook his head. Even now, knowing what he knew about CJD, he still could not quite believe how fast that disease had progressed. Ken had seemed fine. Until he wasn't. And his family had felt as though they'd missed out on saying goodbye, because Ken hadn't been conscious enough to realise.

But Eli believed Ken knew. That he'd heard. Because he did believe that the hearing was one of the last senses to go and that, even though Ken couldn't respond, he heard his family say 'I love you'.

'This will be your room.' Eli stepped back, so Charlie could go in and take a look around. He watched her carefully. Observing her facial expression. The way she moved. The way she now looked. She was a couple of years younger than him, but he'd known, even back then, that she would grow up to be beautiful. He'd just not anticipated *how* beautiful. The acne had gone and now her skin was smooth and soft. Long, thick chestnut-coloured hair. Wide brown eyes, beautiful high cheekbones and full, soft lips. She was elegant. Maybe a little too thin still? But she'd always been highly strung. An anxious mess of nerves as a kid. Maybe she was still the same and living off nervous energy all the time?

Charlie trailed fingertips across her desk, then

stopped and frowned, reaching to pick up the large plastic frog he'd left on top of her computer. 'Really, Eli?'

He couldn't help but chuckle. Glad she'd noticed it. Happy that she'd remembered the reference. 'Just a reminder of happy times past.'

'Happy times past? You should give me the dictionary you're using because I don't think happy times past means what you think it means.'

'Oh, come on, the frog thing was funny.'

She stared at him, no hint of humour on her face. 'For you, maybe.' She threw the plastic frog into the trash can underneath the desk.

Okay, so maybe leaving a live frog in her bed as a parting gift before he left with the Clarks wasn't the greatest thing to do, but he'd been scared! As an orphan, you always hoped the day would come in which you'd finally get a family, but then when you did, it was terrifying, because what if those people weren't what you hoped they'd be? The Clarks had seemed great and he'd got along fantastic with them, but what if it was all for show? What if they weren't who they seemed to be? Other kids kept coming back because it hadn't worked out. Some kids came back because the police had got involved. Eli was having to say goodbye to the one family he did know and he wanted everyone, including Charlie, to remember him. And as he'd joked around and pranked her before, he figured another prank was the way to go!

It was his way of saying *I'm gonna miss you, kid.*

There was a pond near to the orphanage and on the day he knew he was going to go away with the Clarks, he sneaked out quickly after breakfast with everyone and caught the frog. It might even have been a toad. Ugly little thing it was, brown and lumpy, and he tucked it into her bed, down near the foot end, knowing she made her bed every day after breakfast. He could have put that frog in anyone's bed, but he put it in hers, because...well, he didn't know why.

He hoped to be around to see her find it. To give her a hug and say goodbye, but the Clarks made good time in the traffic and they arrived early and so he never got to see her reaction...

I guess she didn't enjoy it.

'Is this how it's going to be every day, while I'm here?' she asked.

'Maybe not *every* day.' He tried to say it as a joke, but it landed on deaf ears. She didn't find it funny and it left him feeling a little frustrated, but he chose not to show it.

'I'm here to do a job, Eli. Not have a replay of our childhood years, which for you might have been great fun, but for me they're not something I choose to recall with fondness. I'd appreciate it if you'd just let me do my job and not tell other people about how you know me.'

Well, it might be a little late for that. Because his family knew. He'd told them already when he'd recognised her name on the information sent over by the agency. 'All right.'

She nodded. 'Good.'

A buzzer sounded. A short, sharp sound.

She looked up. 'What's that?'

Eli smiled. Saved by the bell. 'It means we have a patient in the clinic.'

'Great.'

'Follow me.' He led the way back to his consulting room, a room he loved and adored.

His walls were covered in photographs that he'd taken. The beauty of Vasquez. The landscape. The wild animals. A grizzly catching salmon. A moose scratching its head on a tree. An osprey that had just caught a large trout. But then there were all the other photos. Eli on a parachute jump in mid-air. Eli paddle-boarding on Vasquez Lake. Another of him hand-feeding a wolf cub. Then there were the trophies that lined his cabinets. First place in that chainsaw competition he'd participated in. Second place for most fish caught in an ice-fishing competition. Fastest ascent on Rainier's Peak. Third place in the 2022 Vasquez Ironman Race. A medal for coming tenth in an extreme one hundred K race.

'Are these all yours?' she asked in surprise.

'Just a few that I keep on display.'

'There's *more*?'

'You should see my house.' He grinned, thinking of his trophy room. It was silly really, but it was something his new mom had started when they'd adopted him. Every achievement he ever had, she either made him a certificate or got him a gift. If he got a high score on an essay. When he got into college. When he learned to drive. When he got accepted into medical school. He'd thought she was just being cute, but then he'd realised he really began to value the recognition that he'd achieved something, that he was good at something, and it drove him to join clubs and societies.

At med school, everyone thought that he might fail because so much of his spare time was taken up doing sports or something. But he not only passed, he was top of his year. He had so many friends, so many dudes he knew he could rely on. So much female attention it was almost embarrassing. But he'd never been so admired or loved before and it was heady. Being active, engaging in extreme sports and testing himself became a way for him to feel good about himself. Especially after the cancer. These things, these trophies, they became proof that he was still who he wanted to be. Loved. *Able*. In every way except the one way he craved.

Eli swiped his ID card through the reader and

tapped some details into the computer to bring up the patient who had arrived in clinic.

'Camille Henriksen. Injury to hand' was what it said on the screen. Could be anything.

'First patient is Camille. Fine ol' gal. Must be ninety, if she's a day. Came here with her husband over fifty years ago.'

Charlie nodded.

Eli went to call his patient and stood in the doorway waiting for her. When she came shuffling into view, he noticed that she had a dish towel wrapped around her left hand that looked bloody. 'Camille, what have you done to yourself this time?'

'Oh, I was just cleaning some fish that Marv brought back and the knife slipped. I'm sure it's just a small nick, but Marv insisted I come because I ain't had my tetanus in a while.'

'All right, well, you come on in and take a seat and we'll have a look. I got our new temporary doctor in here with me observing, Dr Charlie Griffin, is that okay with you?'

Camille looked in at Charlie and smiled and tried to wave with her bloodied towel. 'Hello, Charlie. Always nice to see a new face around here.'

'Pleasure to meet you, Mrs Henriksen.'

'Oh, call me, Camille. Everyone does.' Camille shuffled over to the patient's seating area and sat down with a heavy breath. 'Whoo! That's quite the walk. I'm getting my steps in today.'

Eli grabbed some gloves, passed a pair to Charlie and then sat opposite Camille after he'd assembled some gauze pads, a saline wash and some proper bandaging on a small trolley. 'Let's see what we've got here. You okay for me to unwrap this?'

'You do what you have to, Eli, I'm a tough ol' bird.'

'You're a sprightly young thing, Camille. Less of the old,' he said with a smile, playing the game they always played when Camille mentioned her age.

She smiled back at him, wincing slightly as he got closer to the injury.

The dish towel was soaked with blood. And he knew his patient was always dramatically reducing the description of her illnesses and injuries. Once she'd mentioned she was a little hot and she'd been running a fever of a hundred and two. Another time she'd complained about *a bit of a rash* she had and it had turned out she'd had the worst case of shingles he'd ever seen! Considering the amount of blood, he knew he wasn't about to see *a small nick*. Whatever she'd done, he expected to be putting in stitches. The question was, how many?

He unwrapped the final part of the towel and kept his face neutral, but he heard Charlie suck in a small gasp. The *small nick* was her missing the top half of her left index finger!

'Camille…'

'It ain't that bad. You just stitch me up and give me my shot and I'll be on my way.'

'Where's the fingertip, Cam?' he asked.

She grimaced slightly. 'Well, that's a bit of a story in itself.'

'Tell me.'

'It rolled off the chopping board and onto the floor and you know Sookie, you know what she's like when I'm in the kitchen preparing food, she's always there. Watching. Waiting.'

'Who's Sookie?' Charlie asked.

'My Labrador. Been with me eight years.' Camille smiled with fondness. 'Anyway, she might have run off into the garden with it and by the time I'd wrapped my hand and got out there to take it off her, it was all mangled and chewed and so I had to throw it away.'

'It's in the garbage?' asked Eli.

''Fraid so. There'd have been no point in bringing it along here anyways, so just you stitch me up and send me on my way. I've still got that mess to clean in the kitchen and my Marv don't like to wait for his dinner.'

'Marv can make his own dinner just this once. I can't just stitch you up, Camille. I've got to clean this out and somehow join up the edges. I might need to do a small skin graft or create a skin flap.'

'Sounds expensive.'

'Sounds *necessary*,' he replied in a sterner voice, knowing he needed to let her know that they couldn't just rush this or put a sticking plaster on it.

Camille sighed. 'I'm gonna be here a while?'

'You're gonna be here a while,' he answered, this time with understanding and sympathy. He glanced at Charlie. She was listening and watching intently. 'Listen, I'll give Marv a ring, explain the situation and, if he's really put out, I'll get someone to go to your place with a sandwich or something. What do you say?'

Camille smiled and patted Eli's cheek with her good hand. 'You're a good boy to me.'

He cradled her hand with his own. 'You make it easy. Now then. Let me clean this and bandage it up so a nurse can get you to X-Ray. Afterwards you can sit in the TV room for a while, all right?'

'All right.'

He made quick work of cleaning and dressing her wound then got up and went over to his desk. Lifted the phone and punched in a number. 'Hi, yeah, can you send Diana through to take Camille to X-Ray? Cheers.' He put down the phone. 'The nurse is going to take you to X-Ray, just to make sure you haven't chipped the bone.'

Camille nodded and then shuffled away with the nurse after she arrived.

He turned back to Charlie with a smile. 'Yes, before you ask. They're all like that here.'

'She just seemed fine with the idea that she'd lost the top of her finger.' Charlie was helping him clear away the debris left behind by him re-dressing Camille's wound. 'What do you think she'll prefer?'

He thought for a minute. 'Knowing Camille? Local anaesthetic and a skin flap, so she can get home quicker. If the bone isn't damaged, we can just clean it back a little, remove the rest of the nail and stitch the skin into position. Want to as-sist?'

'Yes, of course.'

'Ever done one of these before?'

'Yes, but it was a full finger amputation, though.'

'Great.' He went to write up his notes on Ca-mille, his fingers racing over the keyboard. A new file popped up in the corner of his screen and when he accessed it, he saw it was Camille's X-ray. 'Tell me what you see.' He knew she was qualified. More than qualified. Charlie had had experience in many different centres, primary care clinics and emergency rooms, but he still wanted to assess her skill.

Charlie came behind him and leaned forward to look at the screen, her long brown hair brushed over his shoulder and he couldn't help but in-hale her scent. It was something soft. Feminine.

Meadow-like? It did delicious things to his insides and he had to silently inhale a long, slow breath.

'Looks clean to me. The bone hasn't been damaged. The distal phalanx looks complete. Some signs of arthritis, but that's to be expected in a woman her age.'

'I agree. Okay. Let's go offer Camille an upgrade.'

Eli looked different in scrubs and, with his hair tied back and a face mask on, all she could see were his eyes smiling at her from across their patient.

It was an unsettling thing being smiled at by Eli. The shared knowledge of their history beamed out from every glance, every twinkle, every crease of his eyes when he laughed or joked and tried to include her. His smile said *I Know You* and all she could feel was fear, because of it. She didn't like people knowing her. She didn't like people getting close. She preferred to be an unknown entity.

Camille was more than happy with the treatment plan and had clutched Charlie's hand intensely as Eli had injected the ring block to numb Camille's finger completely.

Ring blocks were painful, because the needle had to be inserted in sensitive areas at the base of the finger where it met the palm and also had to be inserted a couple of times, on both sides to ensure that the correct nerves were anaesthetised, so that the procedure could be completed painlessly.

'All done,' Charlie said, smiling, dabbing away at the spots of blood that had appeared.

'I think that hurt more than chopping the tip off,' said Camille.

'You just lie back now and think of something nice,' said Eli. 'Think of lying on a nice warm beach, cocktail in one hand and a damn fine book in the other.'

'Hah!' said Camille. 'I'd rather think of a handsome young man wafting me with an ostrich-feather fan. Is that okay, or am I being sexist?'

'You think of whatever you want,' said Charlie, smiling. She liked Camille. The lady was feisty and funny and brave, with a kick-ass attitude to life that Charlie wished she could have. 'You don't want to think of Marv wafting you with a fan?'

'Oh, honey, where's the fun in that? I've seen my husband without a shirt and, though I love him dearly, I'd much rather think of a strongly muscled torso, if you don't mind?'

Charlie couldn't help but remember the sight of Eli half naked doing press-ups in his office and how the sight of *him* had affected *her*.

Eli chuckled. 'Whatever works.'

Thinking of Eli's muscles certainly worked to help fire Charlie's imagination! He'd changed from a tall, lanky teen to a hunk of edible proportions who'd look more at home doing a calendar shoot.

Physically, he'd changed, that was for sure. But mentally? Emotionally? He still seemed like a prankster. A joker. Someone who always saw the lighter side of life, who was always on the lookout for laughs. And that made him dangerous, because she'd had enough of humiliation. Was too sensitive to it.

Maybe he ought to have pursued a life as a stand-up comedian? Because he'd never mentioned wanting to be a doctor. She'd have remembered that conversation. Becoming a doctor was all Charlie had ever wanted to do and she'd adored watching the medical dramas on the TV as a young kid, imagining herself doing the same kind of work. Saving lives. Making a difference.

The human body was amazing. It had a vast amount of different systems within, it had millions of different things that could go wrong with it. Diseases, conditions, bacteria, viruses, genetics, accidents. Sometimes it was a mystery, but, mostly, problems could be resolved and people walked away better. Healthier. Happier. Her entire childhood, she'd felt insignificant. As if she wasn't important and becoming a doctor would make her feel as though she did have a purpose. That what she did mattered. That she *was* important.

She'd never expected to become a mother so quickly, but it had happened, and when she'd given birth to Alice and held her in her arms? She'd known that she mattered now, more than anything. Her daughter needed her. Relied on her. Loved her. Unconditionally. And that love was such an overwhelming force! She no longer felt like a nobody.

That fascination with the human body had then terrified her, because she knew of all the horrible things that could possibly assail her daughter and there might be something that she wouldn't be able to save Alice from. That was what kept her up at night and staring at the ceiling and occasionally creeping into her daughter's room to check on her and stare at her and feel love for her ooze from every pore. And then, when Glen had done what he did…she'd realised all the other dangers that Alice might face in her future, too.

Eli worked quickly. Deftly. Chatting with Camille to keep her calm, making her laugh, making her smile. Doing the thing that Eli did best.

'You hear about Abe being knocked into the bay by a laker?' He chuckled.

'Laker?' Charlie frowned, not sure of the term.

'It's a fish. A lake trout.' Camille smiled. 'And no, I hadn't. What happened?'

'He was out fishing and got a bite. Stood up to reel it in, not realising he'd got a whopper on the other end. Damn thing fought him tooth and nail, he said, and, with all the lunging and fighting, knocked Abe off balance and he fell into the bay. Said it was a forty-pounder, at least.'

Camille laughed. 'Hah! Typical of Abe. I bet it was tiny, but he fell into the bay because of how many beers he'd been drinking.'

'Couldn't say for sure. He didn't come in here afterwards for a check-up, but his wife told me he came home soaking wet with a tall tale to tell.'

'Sounds like Abe!'

Charlie smiled, listening. Everyone seemed to know everyone here and maybe that was a good thing in such an isolated spot? Maybe it wasn't. What about having some privacy? 'Did he bring home the fish?' she asked.

Eli met her gaze and she was hit by the impact of it. It made her feel warm and gooey inside and that disturbed her greatly, so she looked away, breaking eye contact to reach for another gauze pad. 'No. Said we all needed to take his word for it. Now he's obsessed with going out there every day to catch his giant laker. Says it might be a record-breaker.'

'Maybe he's telling the truth,' she suggested.

Camille smiled at her in that way that told Charlie she was being naive. 'Once you've met Abe, then maybe you'll reassess your position on that one.'

'I do like to make my own mind up on people. Not just listen to what others say. Who's to know their reason for telling a story a certain way?'

They both looked at her.

'Fair enough,' said Eli. 'You're absolutely right.'

She smiled, glad to have made her point.

'But we're right, too.' He grinned at her and continued tying off the last stitch, snipping the stitch free with his scissors. 'All done! Gonna get this bandaged up now, then give you your tetanus shot, okay?'

'Okay.'

'We're gonna need you to keep this dry as much as you can and come back in ten days to have the stitches removed. I'll book you in an appointment now. But if you have any pain, or develop any fever or feel unwell, I want you to call immediately, okay?'

'I know, I know. This ain't my first time at a rodeo.'

When Camille had gone home, they returned to the clinic to discover there were two more people waiting patiently. One was sitting with a laptop, furiously writing away with what looked like a large sticking plaster, leaking blood, stuck to the side of her face, and the other was a guy sitting with one gloriously swollen ankle propped up on a chair.

Charlie looked at Eli and whispered, 'Is everyone accident-prone, here in Vasquez? Does anyone turn up with, say, a sore throat?'

Eli smiled at her. 'What do you think?'

CHAPTER FOUR

WHEN CHARLIE COLLECTED her daughter from kindergarten, Alice came running out, happily clutching a painting she'd done of two figures in purples, reds and greens. 'Look what I did!' she said, showing her mom the art.

'That's amazing! Is that me and you?' Charlie asked.

'No, that's me and Mrs Clark, my teacher!'

'Oh. Lovely.' She tried not to act surprised. They'd been here in Vasquez five minutes and by all accounts the Clark family owned most things round here and already Mrs Clark, Eli's mother, had usurped Charlie's position in Alice's drawings. Was this teacher superwoman? She had to be bloody amazing to have inspired this.

Trying not to let it bother her, she walked Alice home, her daughter chatting all the way about what her first day had been like. Apparently kindergarten was *the best*.

She was happy for her. Truly. But this was the first time Charlie had spent so much time away from her daughter and she was already beginning to feel a little displaced. A part of her had hoped that Alice would have missed her and they'd spend this time walking home and making something for the potluck together, so that they could soak up being with each other again, but Alice seemed like a new child.

I mean, it's great. I love that she's so independent. I raised her to be that way, of course.

But was it backfiring?

Who is the only person you can rely on?
Me!

Who is the only person who can make you happy?
Me!

Had Charlie inadvertently ingrained into her daughter that she couldn't even rely on her own mother? Because that was not what she'd intended the mantras to mean. She'd meant that Alice couldn't rely on anyone else *except* her. That *she* could still make her daughter happy.

Charlie bit her lip as she unlocked the door to the cottage and let them in. 'We're going to a potluck tonight at Mrs Clark's house.'

'We are?' Alice looked thrilled and began bouncing around the house. 'That's amazing! She's so great, Mom!'

'So I keep hearing.' She gave a bit of a rictus grin and then turned to open the fridge and examine the contents. 'What do you think we should make?'

'PB and J sandwiches.'

Charlie smiled. 'You don't take sandwiches to a potluck, honey. You cook something. Take something hot.'

'Oh.'

'I could do chicken enchiladas? You fancy those?'

'Great! Can I go outside and play until then?'

'Sure, honey.' The cottage came with a small but pretty enclosed garden, with a six-foot wooden fence at the back that offered some protection from the forest and mountains that rose up behind it. Charlie felt sure that she'd be safe out there. There was no pond to worry about, no rockery for her to fall on and crack her head open—which was what the woman with the laptop had done, needing two stitches for her trouble. The cottage had simple flower beds and a lawn. That was it.

Charlie began chopping onions, peppers and chillies, while a pan gently warmed on the hob, then she set them to frying, while she cut the chicken breasts into small chunks.

She tried not to think of Eli. She tried even harder not to think of Alice's painting stuck to the fridge by magnets, of her daughter and her kindergarten teacher. One day at school and already the effusively warm Mrs Clark had taken Charlie's place in her daughter's affections.

It seemed unfair. It seemed wrong and, Charlie had to admit, she felt a little jealous about it. An ugly emotion she didn't like feeling.

Stirring the refried beans into the passata and sweetcorn, she mused on the day and what it had been like to work with Eli. Apart from the half-naked workout and the frog reminder, it hadn't gone too badly. Clearly Eli was liked by his patients, who all seemed on first-name terms with him, which seemed odd. Charlie was used to being addressed as Dr Griffin. She liked that. It helped establish a professional distance from the patient and she'd worked hard to get the Dr part before her name. Hearing patients calling her Charlie had seemed weird.

'Eli' was a talented doctor, who stitched neatly despite the size of his large hands, who was adept with a scalpel and listened to his patients and involved them with their medical choices and options. He was still as ebullient as ever. Always looking for the joke, always grinning that cheeky grin of his, which she had to admit was actually kind of hot, and so the only two issues she had to face with him were the facts that he knew too much about her and that he was insanely attractive.

But she could never get involved with someone like Eli. Absolutely no way! She had a daughter to think about for one, and her daughter's father had humiliated her to such a level that she could never think of being with anyone else, never mind Eli, who thought that looking for laughs was the way to live life. She didn't need someone like that in her and Alice's life. Men were off-limits big-time. She had no time for them any more. It was just going to be herself and Alice from now on.

Unless Alice runs off with the amazing Mrs Clark.

On the walkover to the Clarks' house, Charlie was giving Alice the rules. 'We're not going to stay long, okay? It's a school night for one and I don't want you out too late. And remember, this is your teacher's house, so you call her Mrs Clark at all times. Once we've been there an hour, we're going to leave, okay?'

'Only an hour, Mom?'

'Alice, please…'

'Okay.' Alice didn't sound thrilled, but agreed. Clearly she had wonderful ideas about learning all about Mrs Clark by exploring her house and holding her teacher's hand all night, without letting go, because she was her *'new, most favouritest teacher ever!'*

The Clark house was the biggest in Vasquez. Of timber construction and painted white, it looked to be only a few years old. A new build? Maybe. The lawns were neatly trimmed and the front porch had a swing seat, lanterns and pots of beautiful flowers that Charlie couldn't name.

A chocolate Labrador watched them approach up the front pathway, thumping its wagging tail against the floorboards.

'Mom, look! A doggy!' Alice let go of her hand and tried to dash forward, forgetting everything Charlie had ever told her about the dangers of unknown dogs. She managed to grab Alice before she could get to it.

Of course the Clarks would have a dog. Of course it would be the cutest, friendliest-looking dog Charlie had ever met. Because for the last year, Alice had been begging her for a dog. She'd bought Alice dog plushies and always answered with *'One day, baby, not yet...'* and Alice would pout and frown and whine.

So, of course the perfect Clarks would have a dog. Why wouldn't they?

'It might not be friendly.' She tried to warn her daughter, as she always did when they were out and about in the world. Strange dogs could never be trusted, Alice should know that.

The front door that was hung with a handmade sign, adorned with ribbons and dried flowers that said *Welcome!* on it, opened and out stepped Mrs Clark with a beaming face. 'Hey, Alice! That's okay, you can give Mitch a cuddle! He loves cuddles.'

Charlie let go and her daughter ran the last few steps to the dog, knelt and threw her arms around it as Mitch proceeded to lick her face as if she were a lamb chop.

'Alice, don't let it—'

But it was too late. Alice was giggling and chuckling as Mitch slobbered all over her.

Mrs Clark smiled. 'Hello, Charlie. Mitch's tail is kind of like an early warning system here. As soon as we hear it thumping on wood, we know someone's coming. How are you, my dear?' Mrs Clark leaned forward and dropped a surprising kiss of welcome on Charlie's cheek. She stood back and waited for a response.

'I'm good, thanks. Alice had a great first day, by all accounts.'

'And did you?' Mrs Clark slipped her arm through Charlie's. 'You must come in and tell me all about it. Eli's told me his version, but I want to hear all about it from you.'

'Eli's here?' She stopped abruptly, surprised as to why she didn't consider that Eli might be at his mother's potluck.

'Of course! Now come on in and tell me all about it. Alice, sweetheart? Why don't you bring Mitch in and I'll find you some treats to feed him?'

And before Charlie could protest or say she'd changed her mind about coming, Mrs Clark was sweeping her into the house, saying, 'And you must call me Gayle.'

The Clark house had that warm and inviting

cottage look. Lots of floral prints and soft, pale
stripes on cushions and rugs. Cream-coloured
lamps lit pastel-painted bookcases, filled with
leather-bound books. Huge, soft sofas adorned the
living space, and next to one sat a wicker basket,
filled with hand-wound balls of wool and what
looked like a hat mid-make on a set of circular
needles. Charlie knew they were called that, because a few years back she'd decided to try to
knit Alice a jumper and the lady in the shop had
told her that circular needles and using the magic
loop method was the best way to do so, because
then the jumper wouldn't have side seams. Well,
Charlie had got hopelessly lost and the jumper, or
what there was of it, had ended up being stuffed
in a bag and donated to a craft library. A huge
waste of money, but at least she had tried, hoping
it would give her something to do after Alice was
in bed and she had to sit alone in an apartment,
pondering her life.

There were lots of people standing around that
Charlie didn't know and Gayle lost no time in in-
troducing her to everyone. A sea of names was
given—mostly Clark relations—and she had no
hope of remembering who was who, or who was
a cousin, or an aunt or a nephew, but she saw
Alice brush past her, being taken to the back garden to play with a bunch of other kids and Mitch.
She wanted to tell her to be careful, but her voice
got stuck in her throat, because suddenly Eli was

there, holding a bottle of beer and looking ravishing in a soft off-white linen shirt and jeans.

'Hey.'

She awkwardly felt her cheeks colour. 'Hi.'

'It must be lovely to be reunited after all these years,' said Gayle. 'You two must have *so much* to talk about! Let me get you a drink, Charlie. What would you like?'

'Just an orange juice, if you have one, thanks.'

'You don't want anything stronger? We have wine?'

'I don't drink.'

'All right, orange juice it is. Let me take that, it looks wonderful!' and Gayle disappeared with her chicken enchilada dish, through the throng of people.

Charlie looked at the assembled guests, feeling awful. 'Is this a party? A birthday or an anniversary? Am I missing something? Should I have brought a gift?'

'Nope. Just a little get-together.'

'*Little?* You and I have different dictionaries.'

He laughed. 'This is just what it's like here. This is what having a family is like.'

'Is it?' She crossed her arms in front of her, feeling uncomfortable. She wasn't used to this! She'd never been part of anything this large. Even when she was married! Her husband hadn't had any close family. Even when they'd married it had just been a couple of witnesses at City Hall.

'Look, I know you're still feral and all, but try to relax. Enjoy it!'

She looked straight at him. 'I'm not feral!'

'Aren't you? I've seen more confident looks in cats backed into a corner.'

'I'm not feral. I know how to be around people.'

'But you don't know how to be comfortable around people who want to know more about you. I saw it today. You were taken aback when a patient called you Charlie, instead of Doctor. When people close the distance, your hackles go up. I can tell just by looking at you. Standing there with your arms crossed and looking for the exits with that frightened look upon your face. Relax a little. No one's going to bite you.' He took a swig from his bottle of beer.

She hated that he could tell! So she uncrossed her arms, but then she didn't know how to stand all of a sudden, without something to do with her hands, so she crossed her arms again.

Eli chuckled.

'Shut up!'

He laughed some more and she wanted to turn tail in that moment, find Alice and get the hell out of there!

But wouldn't that be proving his point?

So she wasn't great at people being close, so what? Eli had led a different life from hers. Their paths had diverted when he'd got adopted into the Clark family. Hers had continued to be hard, lonely and painful.

'I'm trying my best,' she said quietly.

And he looked at her in that moment, in this strange, intense way, so that she imagined he could somehow see all that had happened to her, every moment of hardship and humiliation, and she felt naked beneath his gaze.

'Here you go! One orange juice. Now then, Eli, don't monopolise Charlie! I want to introduce her to Gran.' Suddenly Gayle was pulling her away from the heat of Eli's gaze and through the crowds once again, into the kitchen this time to be introduced to a tiny silver-haired lady, who wore an apron and seemed to be deeply involved in the mass production of chocolate-chip cookies.

'Gran? This is Charlie, Eli's friend and new colleague at the clinic.'

Charlie extended a hand, but Gran looked at her oddly and stepped forward for a hug, instead.

'Hello, Charlie. Short for Charlotte, is it?'

Surprised by the sudden hug, she squeezed back and, when she was released, nodded, with a smile. 'Yes, that's right.'

'I always wanted to call Gayle Charlotte, but my husband—*may he rest in peace*—didn't like it and so Gayle it was. Eli never told us you were a pretty little thing.'

She wasn't sure how to respond to that. To be pleased that Gran thought she was pretty, or upset that Eli hadn't mentioned it? Not that she needed him to notice, but she worked hard to try and look good. She worked out at home often. Yoga. Pilates. Cardio twice a week. She ensured she always had her hair done every ten weeks and tried to eat healthily. But she wasn't doing it for any man. She did it for herself, for her own strive to perfection. Sometimes, she overdid it. Punishing herself with harsh exercise and high-intensity interval workouts. The last time had been after Glen had...

No. She didn't want to think about that again. It had already occupied too much of her life and decisions.

'Do you bake, Charlie?'

'Er, sometimes.'

'What's your favourite dessert? There's only one right answer, now!'

Panicked under the sudden pressure, she squeaked out an answer. 'Apple pie?'

Gran stared at her for a moment, then chuckled, slapping Charlie on the arm. 'Perfect! You're a keeper, for sure! Now, why don't you help me with the next batch?'

The next hour or so whizzed by in a whirlwind of flour, eggs and chocolate chips. Gran shared all her secrets—a pinch of cinnamon and nutmeg—and talked non-stop while they were in the kitchen.

At first, Charlie felt a little uncomfortable, but

after a while she relaxed into it and laughed and chuckled at Gran's stories of her early years romancing her soon-to-be husband, George, and how he'd sneak up the trellis at nights to knock on her bedroom window and sneak a kiss, and all the romance of their midnight escapes to take a walk beneath the moon and stars, hand in hand. Sometimes, Charlie just stood there and listened, not realising that she had been whisked away into a world of old-fashioned romance and wooing and how much she yearned for the world to be as simple as it was many decades ago. If you made a mistake relationship-wise back then, hardly anyone knew about it. Today? In this modern world? With social media being so prolific? You could be plastered across anyone's page in seconds, for the whole world to see. Until the end of days.

She didn't realise that Eli had been standing in the kitchen doorway watching her, until he spoke. 'Time to eat.'

Charlie turned, blushing, pulled back into the present, and she washed her hands, drying them on a towel. 'How can I help?' she asked.

'You've helped plenty. You're a guest. Gran? You shouldn't have worked her so hard…she's already had a long day.'

'Nonsense, Eli! This girl's got spirit. Now, Charlie, why don't you help me take these cookies through?'

She was happy to help. In fact, she liked helping and feeling a part of them. She wasn't sure how it had happened. One minute she'd been feeling trapped, the next she was revelling in the warmth of them all. This family group. And though, technically, she was an outsider, she'd been made to feel welcome. To feel an honorary member of this family. Even if it was just for this night. Gran had made her feel secure, as if she'd known that Charlie didn't want to answer personal questions, and so Gran had kept her questions light. What sports team did she follow? What was her favourite music? Had she seen last night's episode of some soap that Gran liked to watch?

At the rear of the house was a large porch that had a few long picnic tables set up, which was slowly beginning to groan with food, and, around the tables, all the gathered Clark family, her and Alice. Her daughter was at the far end, chuckling with kids her own age, and Charlie smiled to see her look so happy as she slid into a seat between Gayle and Eli. There didn't seem to be any standing on ceremony, everyone just dived into whatever food they fancied, and she couldn't help but notice that Eli loaded up his plate with her chicken enchiladas, a huge forkful of a green salad and a couple of dinner rolls. Charlie helped herself to some pasta that looked to be mixed with a spicy sausage of some kind and peppers, along with a different salad that was decorated with bacon bits and herby croutons.

'This is delicious,' she said to Gayle. 'How often do you guys get together like this?' She expected her to say that they didn't do it very often.

'All the time! Birthdays, anniversaries, graduations, days that end in the letter Y!' Gayle laughed and took a sip of her drink.

'Really? Isn't it a lot of hard work?'

'No! It's fun! Family is the most important thing in the world and, when you have it, you need to celebrate it as often as you can. Show people that you love them and want them around. That you're there as a supportive network for anything.' Gayle leaned in. 'Life is hard, you know? We know that more than most. But no one has to walk their path in life alone. With family? You can be strong and no matter what the world throws at you, it can't bring you down.'

Charlie smiled, slightly awestruck by the difference in their lifestyles. The Clarks clearly believed that together they were a force to be reckoned with, whereas Charlie had raised Alice to believe in the fact that they stood alone in this world and they could rely only on themselves. Who was right and who was wrong?

'Having family and having love is something you want to share. It's useless on its own when we all have so much love to give. That's why we decided we'd adopt. There are so many kids in this world that just need a chance, you know?'

Charlie nodded.

'Our lives have been so enriched since we brought Eli into our fold. Even through all his trials and tribulations, we wouldn't have had it any other way.'

His trials and tribulations? Surely his life had been perfect?

'We were pulled into his orbit. I mean…how could we not be? Have you seen him? He's gorgeous! But no, seriously, when you know, you know. Eli's vitality for life is infectious. He's always smiling, or laughing, and when we spoke to him, we just gelled, you know? You must know, you knew him back then!'

Yes, she'd known him. And Gayle was right. He did have and still had a vitality for life and seeking joy, but she hadn't known how to deal with him back then and she wasn't sure she knew how to deal with him now. Sitting this close, being part of his family, being welcomed, made her feel confused. It made her question her own life and what she might have been missing in it. It made her feel sad.

'I did.'

Gayle leaned in, conspiratorially. 'He told us about the frog.' She laughed.

Charlie nodded, smiling. 'He did?'

'Took him till last week to tell us, when he knew you were coming.'

'Did he tell you he put a frog in my office today, too?'

'A real one?'

'Plastic.'

'Eli!' Gayle scolded him and he chuckled beside her. Clearly happy to have surprised his mom and made her smile.

His *mom*.

He truly had been accepted as a member of this family. He was one of them, that was clear, the adoption was just paperwork. Eli was a Clark, through and through.

Charlie had always been sceptical of what it might feel like to be adopted. Whether you would truly feel a part of someone else's family. Whether they would accept you and treat you the same as their actual blood relatives.

But it had happened here, or so it seemed. Maybe Eli was just so laid-back and chill about everything, he didn't stress about it the way she once had?

Did she need to take a leaf out of Eli's book?

She couldn't believe she was even having to consider it.

CHAPTER FIVE

HE'D BEEN FOR his usual ten-kilometre run and was just arriving at the clinic in his running gear of sleeveless grey vest and red shorts when he noticed Charlie arriving with Frank Schwarz.

Charlie appeared to be trying to escort Frank into the building, but Frank was having none of it, slapping away Charlie's efforts to get him inside.

'Now, hold your horses there, missy!'

'Sir? You need to come inside, so I can treat you!'

'Hold up! Hold up, Charlie. This is Frank, he doesn't like going into hospitals or clinics.'

'But he's hurt!' she insisted, indicating the large fishing hook piercing his neck.

Eli had noticed the hook already. It had quite the barb poking out of Frank's skin, blood trickling down past his collar and staining his usual blue-checked flannel. 'I know that, but Frank doesn't come inside.'

'Whyever not?'

'Because everyone he's ever loved has gone

into this building behind us and not come out again, plus Frank has quite the phobia about needles.'

Charlie looked at him. 'Oh. I see, but he can't go around with that thing in his neck—it has to come out!'

'*Really?* I was thinking of leaving it in.' He smiled at her and Frank and steered him over towards the bench that was situated out front. 'How'd this happen, Frank?'

'I was prepping *Molly*, moving some fishing gear about, and I slipped on some oil or what have you and when I got up again, realised there was something catching on my collar. I wouldn't have come here at all. Was gonna clip off the barb and yank it out myself. Except this…' Frank gestured at Charlie '…this *lady* insisted. She was very forceful.'

Eli smiled. 'She can be and she was right to do so, Frank, this can't stay in and it's near to some pretty important structures in the neck.'

'You mean my jugular?'

'Or your carotid. Plus that hook's probably not the cleanest thing in the world either, so we're going to need to get you on some antibiotics.'

Frank frowned. 'I don't like taking tablets.'

'Well, you're going to have to, just this once, okay?'

'You can't just snip this thing and yank it out?'

'I'm sure we can, but I'd really like to get a

scan done, first. It does look superficial, but we need to be sure. You hit your head when you fell?'

I don't think so.'

'You lose consciousness?'

'No. I don't want to go inside there, Eli. I lost my Jane in there.'

Jane had been Frank's wife. They'd been married over forty years, until she had a sudden splitting headache, that had turned out to be a burst aneurysm. She died within minutes, before the medical evacuation could be arranged.

'It'll take five minutes, I promise you. Charlie and I will know what we're dealing with and we can get that sorted and have you back to *Molly* before you know it.'

'Who's Molly?' asked Charlie.

'My boat,' answered Frank.

'Oh.'

Eli smiled at Charlie. She looked beautiful today. Mornings agreed with her. Her hair was soft and floaty as she'd not yet tied it back for work and it cascaded over her shoulders like silk. She had a small divot that formed between her eyebrows, like now, when she was concerned, and her eyes looked darker, somehow.

'What do you say, Frank? You'll come in for the scan? Get treated. I'll give you antibiotics that you must take every day for a week and I'll come round to check on the wound in a couple of days. What do you say? I'll throw in a six-pack of beers, too.'

'He shouldn't drink on antibiotics,' Charlie said.

'I'll bring them when his course is over.' Eli smiled at her and winked at Frank, conspiratorially.

Frank gazed at the building behind them, as if considering it. 'On one condition.'

'What's that?'

'That I can sit outside, while I'm waiting. I don't want to feel trapped inside.'

'I'll open up the quad. There's a small garden. A bench. Some ducks have built a nest there next to the pond. You'll have nature.'

Frank considered it and as he did so, Eli's gaze drifted to Charlie.

She looked disbelieving. As if she couldn't quite believe that he was making all of these concessions for a patient. But she had to know that they performed medicine differently up here. It was hard enough getting patients to come in, in the first place. He would make whatever adaptations necessary to ensure they still received first-class treatment.

'Okay.'

Eli grinned. 'Great. Let's get you in, then.'

They got a hesitant Frank to X-Ray and while the radiologist did her thing, Charlie pulled him to one side. 'That man needs a scan, a tetanus shot, antibiotics and surgery that may or may not be minor! You can't let him sit outside in a garden and promise him a beer!'

'Relax! He's going to get the best treatment he will allow me to give him.'

'That *he* will allow *you*?' she scoffed. 'As doctors, it is up to us to give patients the options for treatment that will keep them safe and healthy for as long as possible. I'm sorry that he's scared of hospitals and needles, but I have never heard of a doctor promising to share a six-pack of beer with a patient, as some sort of bribe!'

'No? Maybe you haven't been working in the right kind of hospitals, then?' Eli was not going to be put off by her sterile, big-city ways. It was different out here in Vasquez. Keeping his patients healthy was a journey and it often felt like bargaining, when a lot of them were stubborn as mules and didn't like to admit to weaknesses. It was a tough crowd out here and he'd learned that quickly. Especially when he'd got sick himself. The people out here braved it out. They lifted their chins, squared their shoulders and faced death head-on. Whether that was from the isolation, the extreme winter weather or the wildlife. Or, in his case? Cancer.

Death was everywhere, a constant friend. The people here acknowledged that and they fought that quietly every time they set foot outside their homes. It wasn't so bad right now, what with it being springtime, but as fall approached and winter threatened, the people here hunkered down and looked out for one another. That was what he was doing for Frank. Supporting him. Acknowledging his fear and offering him a trade. That was all. Something for something. The Vasquez way.

'The right kind of hospitals? People need to understand the risks to their health and Frank needs a proper assessment. He had a fall. What caused that? And are you going to take his word that he didn't pass out? He could be lying to get out of here quicker.'

'He could be, but I'll keep an eye on him.'

'What? He needs to be admitted for tests, as well as the procedure to remove that hook from his neck.'

'I get it, I do, and I can pass Frank's boat every day on my morning run and check in on him. It's the best we're going to get with him and you need to understand that.'

'You're too laid-back about this, Eli.'

He smiled. 'And you're too wound up. City life has got you acting all…shrill and brittle.'

'Shrill and brittle?' Her hands went to her hips and he saw an anger flare in her dark chocolate eyes that he liked and was waiting to hear what she said next when the radiologist opened the door and allowed Frank to exit.

'Where's that quad?'

Eli turned to Charlie. 'My esteemed colleague

from Anchorage will show you, Frank. Charlie, why don't you stay with Frank? Sit with him in the garden for a while. Might be nice for both of you to just sit back and relax?'

He saw the frustration in her eyes, but he kept smiling, knowing she wouldn't disagree with him in front of a colleague, and watched her force a polite smile at their patient instead.

'I'll show you. Follow me.'

Eli watched her go. Felt his gaze drop to her shapely behind as she walked away from him towards the quad. She was still the fiery Charlie he remembered from many years ago, but there was something else there, too. Something he didn't remember. Something he didn't recognise. She was scared. And he wondered what of.

And whether he'd be able to protect her from it.

Or whether he was the one causing it?

CHAPTER SIX

IT SEEMED HERE, in Vasquez, that Charlie couldn't walk more than five yards down the street without some local stopping her to say hello or wanting to chat.

It was midweek. Wednesday lunchtime and she'd been given a whole hour for lunch, which quite frankly was something she'd never experienced in the city hospitals. Mostly food was eaten on the run, or sometimes missed completely and she'd try to grab a bite of something if she passed the staff room, gulping it down as she hurried along to her next patient or emergency.

A whole hour felt like luxury and so she'd decided to go out for a walk and get some fresh air. She was greeted by a mailman who seemed to know her name, even though she didn't know him, an older lady waved hello as she wiped the outdoor tables of her diner, and a guy who looked as old as the hills surrounding Vasquez ambled towards her with his walking stick, doffed his cap and said, 'Hello, Charlie. How's everything going?'

'Oh, it's going very well, thank you.' She smiled, felt awkward. 'How are you?'

'Ooh, not bad. Carrying on, as you do.' He winced slightly.

'Are you okay?'

'Bit of heartburn. Just on my way to get some of those antacids.'

Her instincts kicked in and now she noticed other things about this old man. He looked clammy and his colour was off. Of course, he could look like that normally, but she had noticed in the short time that she was here that Vasquez natives all seemed to look quite weathered and healthy, no matter their age. This gent looked somewhat paler.

'How long have you had the heartburn?'

'Came on about an hour ago and the damn thing won't go away.' He winced again and, with his spare hand not holding the stick, he rubbed at his chest. 'Think it's something bad?'

Was he having a heart attack? 'Let's get you in one of these seats for a moment.' She guided him over to one of the diner chairs and sat him down, then placed her fingers on his wrist to check his pulse.

'Everything okay?' The lady who had waved to her earlier came out looking concerned. 'Stewie? You all right?'

So this was Stewie. The frequent flyer. The hypochondriac she'd been warned about. But this didn't seem like anxiety.

Charlie turned around to her. 'Could you call the clinic and let them know that I need them to send someone out to assist me with this gentleman, please? Query MI.'

The woman nodded hurriedly and bustled back inside.

'Okay, Stewie, is it? I need you to look at me and I need you to take nice, steady breaths and remain calm, okay?'

'What's going on?'

'I think you're having a heart attack.'

Stewie raised his eyebrows at her and gulped. 'R-r-really?'

'Do you feel sick? Have you any pain in your jaw, neck or left arm?'

'I guess a little, but it's not bad at all. If I'm having a heart attack, why aren't I on the floor gasping, clutching at my chest?'

'They don't all present the way you see them on TV. Sometimes they're a little like this. Quieter. Less dramatic.'

'Not like me then. Oh.' He rubbed at his chest again and laid his walking stick up against the table. 'I thought it was because I'd eaten too much breakfast this morning. My wife makes excellent biscuits and gravy.'

She smiled at him.

'Guess I was lucky running into you, huh? I promise I wasn't stalking you as a doctor.'

Charlie smiled sympathetically.

'Eli told me you were coming. He's been really excited about it.'

'Yeah?' She was surprised, but also kind of pleased. 'That's nice.'

'He's a good boy. He's looked after me and my wife for years now. It was a shame that he had to go through what he did. It was a nasty business, him just a young man an' all.'

Charlie assumed he meant the orphanage. Having to live in a children's home and not find a family until he was fifteen years old and adopted by the Clarks. 'But he's landed on his feet here,' she said.

'Yeah. The Clarks…they're good people.' Stewie looked at her. 'You seem nice, too.'

'Thank you. So do you.'

At that moment a vehicle arrived and Eli jumped out, with Diana, one of the nurses from the clinic. 'Stewie? When I send my doctors out for lunch break, I expect them to rest, not find patients on the fly.' Eli was already placing an oxygen mask on Stewie's face as the old man chuckled, then he placed his stethoscope in his ears to listen to Stewie's chest.

She caught his quick nod of acknowledgement that Stewie was most definitely having a heart attack. 'Let's get you in the back of the truck and over to the hospital.'

'Will someone call my Joan?'

'I'll do it,' Charlie offered, clambering into the back of the truck with him to hold his hand as Diana got IV access and Eli placed a BP cuff around the old man's arm. He was a sweet old man and, granted, she barely knew him, but he exuded the warmth and friendship that everyone had seemed to give her since arriving here. Even now, in this moment, where his life was hanging in the balance, Stewie was being warm and charming.

'You're a good 'un,' he said, patting her hand with his. 'Don't scare her, will you?'

'I won't, I promise.'

'Your Joan is made of stern stuff. She doesn't scare easily,' Eli said.

Stewie smiled behind the oxygen mask. 'Nigh on fifty years we've been married, you know, and never a cross word between us.'

Charlie smiled at him. That was the dream, wasn't it? To find someone who suited you perfectly. To find someone who loved you deeply every day. Who enjoyed your company. Who was there for you and supported you and adored you. Someone with whom you could live out every day, happily. She'd hoped to have that with Glen, but it had all gone so horribly wrong.

It was the sort of relationship that she'd never

got close to. Her own romantic history being somewhat more…fraught.

'You make sure to tell her I love her.'

'You can tell her that yourself,' Eli said.

But Stewie met her gaze and looked deeply into her eyes and wordlessly begged her to tell his wife what he wanted her to hear. And she saw it in his eyes—he knew. The end was coming.

Charlie knew they would do everything to make sure he got through this, but if Stewie thought he was going to die, then she should also respect his last request, so she nodded and squeezed his hand and mouthed *I will*.

He smiled and then closed his eyes and the ECG monitor suddenly went crazy, beeping out an alarm.

'He's arresting!' Eli said, stepping out of his seat to stand by Stewie and begin compressions. 'How much further, Diana?'

'Less than a minute!'

'Get us there!'

They leapt into action around their patient. Now was no longer the time to hold Stewie's hand. Charlie needed to help and she'd seen enough MIs to know that even when you were right there, with all the equipment, it didn't mean success was guaranteed. Ninety per cent of cardiac arrests in the United States were fatal, which meant you had a one in ten chance of surviving. Those weren't great odds. But Charlie was not one who bet on the odds. At the end of the day they were just numbers and no one could say whether it was pointless or not.

You helped. If someone was dying, you tried to stop it. If someone was flailing, you tried to save them.

She took over compressions as the truck stopped and Eli thrust the doors open and helped manoeuvre the gurney outside, so they could rush it into the clinic. They'd shocked Stewie twice, but he still wasn't responding and as they rushed into the clinic, alarms blaring from the machines, his rhythm changed from ventricular fibrillation to asystole.

Flatline.

You couldn't shock a flatline.

She kept pushing.

Chest compressions, chest compressions, chest compressions.

One, two, three, four...

Eli pushed epinephrine, but nothing was happening and Stewie's walking stick that had been laid on the gurney next to him fell to the floor with a clatter. It was like a sign that it was no longer needed. Final.

Charlie checked the clock. He'd been asystole for far too long. She caught Eli's eye as Eli stepped back and went over the history of the case, rounds completed, drugs given and how long Stewie had been down for in an unshockable rhythm, with no change. 'I think we should stop. Does everyone agree?'

Charlie continued to do CPR. She would not stop unless everyone agreed and she quickly met everyone's gaze as they all agreed. Stewie would not be coming back.

She stopped. Stood back. Breathless. 'Agreed.'

Eli looked up at the clock. 'Time of death, one twenty-two p.m.' He looked at her. 'Want me to call Joan?'

'No. I said I'd do it.' She was grateful to him for offering but she wanted to be the one. She and Eli left Stewie in the capable hands of the nurses.

'Are you okay?' Eli asked.

'Of course. I've lost patients before. I'll lose them again. This isn't my first time.'

'I know, it's just that here in Vasquez everyone is so close that, when we do lose a patient, we look out for one another. It's not something that just gets forced under the rug, so that you can deal with the next patient and save your tears for when you get home.'

'I didn't know him. Not like you.' She turned to face him. 'Do *you* need to take some time away? I can cover for you, if you like?'

'I'd like to be with you when you tell Joan. I'd like to be there for her. Familiar face and all of that.'

She nodded. 'Okay. If that's what you want.' It was strange to see him so serious, but expected under the circumstances. She was used to the jovial, cheeky Eli. The one with a constant twinkle in his eye, not this.

When Joan arrived, she was taken to a family room and Eli and Charlie followed her in.

'I'm too late, aren't I? I can see it in your faces.' Joan stood staring at them.

Charlie indicated she should take a seat and when she'd sat down, she began to explain. 'I'm so sorry. Your husband suffered a cardiac arrest and despite our best efforts to revive him, I'm afraid he passed away.'

Joan paused, taking it in. 'He just went out for antacids. Said the walk might help his digestion. He had heartburn. It wasn't heartburn?'

Charlie shook her head. 'I'm afraid not.'

'Did he collapse in the street?'

'No. I met him outside the diner and we began to talk. He described his symptoms, which worried me, and I called for an ambulance. We worked hard to revive him, but we were not successful.'

Tears began to well in Joan's eyes.

This was the difficult moment. The moment where Charlie had to be strong and distance herself. Watching other people lose it and become emotional was always a difficult thing for her.

'We almost didn't get together,' Joan said.

Charlie said nothing. If Joan needed to talk to get through this, then she'd let the older woman talk.

'I didn't like him when we first met. He was so full of himself. Good-looking.' She smiled ruefully. 'But he knew it, too. I thought he was playing with me. That he'd asked me out on a dare from his friends, so I said no at first.'

'When did you say yes?' Eli asked.

Joan looked at him, eyes shining with tears. 'Almost five years later. He'd been away, in the army, seeing the world, and when he came back under a medical discharge he came straight to see me. He'd been writing me letters while he was away, telling me that the thought of me was what kept him going, and my feelings for him changed. So I said yes. I wished I'd said yes before, because then I could have had those five extra years with him. We were good together. Never a cross word.'

Charlie smiled. 'He told me that. He also told me that I had to tell you that he loved you. It was the last thing he said. His last thought was of you.' And she envied Stewie and Joan in that moment. To have had such a strong, enduring and powerful love that had spanned decades. They'd been lucky to find such a rare thing.

Joan nodded and sniffed, dabbing at her eyes with a handkerchief. 'I don't know how to live without him. We've never been apart since he came back. How do I do this now?'

'Everyone will help you, Joan. You know that,' Eli said. 'Vasquez won't let you be alone.'

She smiled sadly at him. 'They'll try, but at the end of the day, I'll be alone in our bedroom and one side of the bed will be empty—' Her voice broke on the word 'empty' and she began to sob.

Charlie broke all her rules and draped an arm around Joan's shoulder and Eli mirrored her on the opposite side, their arms touching as they comforted the older woman. She felt his hand graze hers. It was like a lightning strike and she shifted her hand away, her cheeks flaming. She tried to concentrate hard on Joan, but then Eli met her gaze and Charlie couldn't deal with it and stood up abruptly. Not knowing what to say. What to do. What did most people do in this situation?

'I'll get you a strong cup of tea.' She gave a smile to Joan and left the room, glad to be out of such an oppressive, emotional atmosphere. She'd wanted to comfort Joan and she had, but when Eli had mirrored her and his hand had brushed hers, she'd panicked, feeling that they were some-how more and that had scared the living daylights out of her! She was here to work and keep her distance and finish this contract, so she could move on, but Eli had somehow made her feel that she was being pulled further into his orbit and if she got too close, then what? She'd never leave Vasquez? That was an impossibility! That could never happen!

Here in this town, it was as if the Clarks, and Eli, especially, were the sun, And she were Icarus. She could not get too close, or she would get burned. It was just something that she felt implicitly. And she did not want to crash and burn because of him.

In the small kitchenette, she struggled to find tea. There was coffee, but *where was the goddamned tea*? Charlie rummaged through the cupboards, finally finding a box and adding a teabag to a mug. She had no idea if Joan had milk or sugar and so she prepped a small tray. Doing this helped. Being busy helped. Being away from that small room helped. Eli was a big man and his presence in that small room had felt suffocating to her, especially as she'd listened to Joan's story and empathised with her pain over not being with the man she loved for those lost five years.

Why had that story hit Charlie so hard?

She wasn't sure she wanted to examine that too much, if she was being honest with herself. Maybe it was because of the lost chances? Joan's lost five years with Stewie. Charlie's lost chance at being with her own family. Her biological parents, whoever they might be. Her lost chance at a successful marriage. Her lost chance at a successful relationship. Her lost ability to trust anyone. Her lost chance at giving Alice the father she so desperately deserved.

Joan's life was so different from hers. She'd

been with one man and lived in the same place for years and it had been all that she needed.

Charlie had never had that and, though she told herself she didn't need it, maybe she did yearn for the simplicity of that kind of life? Could that ever be hers? Or were she and Alice doomed to be nomads for ever?

She took a slow walk back to the family room and she inhaled a long, deep breath before she knocked lightly and entered.

Eli and Joan were still sitting close together, Eli listening as Joan told a story about her husband.

Charlie laid the tray down on the low coffee table and sat and listened from a chair, away from the sofa that Eli and Joan sat upon. It was strategic. Protection. By distancing herself, maybe she'd get some clarity?

'Is there anyone I can call for you, Joan? Someone who can come and sit with you? Or take you home?'

Joan thought for a moment. 'I guess you could call my neighbour, Connie.'

'I'll get Diana to come and sit with you, until Connie arrives,' said Eli.

He and Charlie left the room together and Eli looked down at her. 'You sure you're okay?'

His concern for her was touching, but it was heady and dangerous, too. 'Absolutely!' She smiled as sweetly as she could, to imply confidence. 'I'll go fetch Diana.' And she turned and walked away from him, her breathing getting easier the further she went.

Eli was out chopping wood for his woodpile when his phone rang. He answered it and heard his mom on the other end of the line.

'Oh, Eli, I'm so glad you answered! I've got a little problem and wondered if you could fix it for me.'

'Sure. What's up?'

'Well, Charlie rang and apparently there's a leaking tap in her kitchen that won't shut off. She's tried to ring Pete, but he's gone to Fairbanks this week to visit his sister.' Pete was the local plumber. 'Could you pop on over to take a look?'

Go to Charlie's? Sure, he could do that. 'No problem. Let her know I'll be over there in about ten minutes.'

'You're a star.'

He laughed. 'I try.' Eli ended the call and put away his axe, after cleaning the blade. He quickly stacked the blocks of wood he'd chopped over on his winter woodpile and then grabbed his flannel shirt and shrugged it on. It was covered in little bits of wood and he brushed them off, grabbing his car keys.

It would be good to see Charlie and Alice again. He'd not seen Charlie's daughter since his mother's potluck, but he had heard about her. His mother had sung the little girl's praises, telling him how clever she was, how good at English and arithmetic she was. How she had a wonderful imagination and was a very neat painter. The little girl excelled, but the one thing his mom had noticed was that Alice pretty much kept to herself at school, the way she had at the potluck. Yes, she'd been with the other children, but she hadn't interacted much, as if she preferred to be by herself. 'I wondered if it's because they move around a lot. Alice told me there's no point in making friends properly, because they always leave,' she'd suggested.

That was odd. 'Maybe. She'll be okay,' he'd said, because Alice's mom was Charlie and Charlie was the most self-sufficient person he'd ever known. She was a strong, capable woman and no doubt she was raising her daughter to be the same way.

He arrived outside her cottage and switched off the engine, getting out of the vehicle and raising a hand in hello at Charlie's next-door neighbour, Angus, who was up a ladder fixing some guttering by the looks of it.

'Leaves?' he called out, trying to guess the blockage.

'Bird nest.'

Eli raised an eyebrow. 'Any eggs?'

'Not yet. Think I should leave it? Or evict them?'

Eli smiled. 'Your call, my friend.' At Charlie's front door, he set down his bag of tools and knocked.

From inside the cottage he could hear music. And then the door was being opened and there stood Charlie. She looked down at the bag as he reached for it.

'You're my plumber, too?'

'Your lucky day, huh?' He liked what she was wearing. She wore a tight-fitting black tee underneath a pair of loose-fitting khaki dungarees and around her hair she had a bright red headscarf. Some of her hair had escaped, loose brown tendrils that hung in gentle waves, and he felt a pang of something that could have been lust, but was most definitely attraction.

'You can fix taps as well as people?'

'Taps are easy.'

'Then you'd better come in.' She stepped back, her cheeks flushing, averting her eyes as he passed and he smiled, glad to know that he was having just as much of an effect on her. It felt good to know he had an effect, because that meant she was just as uncomfortable with the situation as he was.

'Where's Alice?'

'In her room.'

'Has she been bad?'

'No. She just likes to spend time in her room. I think she's drawing, if you want to go say hi.' Clearly she did not expect him to want to say hi.

But he did.

'That'd be great.' He walked down the small corridor that led to the bedrooms, heading to the smaller one of the two and noting Alice's name plaque on the door. He rapped his knuckles against it.

'Come in!'

He pushed open the door. 'Hey, squirt. How are you doing?'

'Eli!' She put down her pencil and ran over to him and he scooped her up and hefted her onto his hip.

'I think you've grown.'

Alice chuckled. 'Want to see my drawing? I'm making a comic.'

'Sure.' He put her down again and she ran over to her table.

Behind him, Charlie leaned on the doorjamb. 'Since when did you two become best friends?'

'Eli showed me some of his funny drawings at that potluck, Mom.'

'Did he, now? What kind of drawings?'

Eli looked up at her. 'Just dogs and chickens and how to sketch in some basic shapes when she wants to create things, so instead of, say, trying to draw a dog's outline from scratch, you think about the shapes first. A rectangle for the body, rectangles for the legs and tail, circles for the neck and head and then how she can construct her drawing on top of those.'

'She's five, Eli.'

He turned to her. 'Your daughter has a gift. Have you seen her drawings?'

'Of course I have!'

He smiled. 'Good. Then you should know that her skill level is way above that of any other five-year-old. You should nurture this.'

He could see in her eyes that she didn't like being told about her daughter in this way. As if he were criticising her for not noticing or something. 'I'm just trying to help, is all.'

'Then come help me in the kitchen. That is what you're here for.' She disappeared from view.

Eli smiled at Alice. 'While I'm fixing that tap, what are you going to draw for me?'

Alice beamed. 'What would you like?'

'How about a dragon?'

'With flames coming out of its mouth?'

'Sounds perfect. See you in a bit.' And he left Alice in her room and made his way to the kitchen, where Charlie was bustling about with mugs.

'Want a coffee?'

'If you're having one.'

He placed his bag of tools down on the floor and examined the kitchen tap. It was indeed dripping quite a lot. 'Probably just needs a new washer fitted. I should have it fixed in no time.'

'Great.'

Eli got busy opening up the cupboard beneath

the sink to find the stopcock that would turn off
the water supply while he worked. Then he stood
and put the plug in the sink. 'Got a spare towel?'

'What for?'

'To place in the sink so I don't scratch it with
anything.'

'Oh, okay.' She passed him a red-and-white-
checked cloth.

Next he began to unscrew the tap.

'Who taught you all of this?' she asked, pouring hot water into two mugs and watching him
closely.

'My dad.'

She nodded. 'Is he a handy guy?'

'Oh, yeah. A man with his fingers in many
pies, but also a guy that likes to be hands on.
When they did up the hotel he could have got in
some tradesmen to do all the work, but he liked
to save some jobs for himself. Plumbing, carpen-
try, electrics. He's a jack of all trades and master
at every one.'

'He seemed a nice guy at the potluck.'

Eli looked at her and smiled. 'He is.'

There was a pause and then she said, 'You really got lucky, huh?'

He unscrewed the valve to access the washer
and nodded, thoughtfully. 'I really did. Did you
miss me when I'd gone?' He meant it as a joke.

But she looked at him oddly. 'Are you kidding
me? It was lovely and quiet without you there. I

could sleep easily without worrying if you'd put itching powder in my socks. I could go sit in the garden and not have you drop a water balloon on me from your room.'

He smiled ruefully at the memories, having forgotten half of the stuff he used to do. It seemed like a lifetime ago and maybe it was. The kids' home belonged to a previous life, almost as if it weren't his at all. But he remembered that day with the water balloon. He'd been messing about with the guys in their dorm and he'd been half soaked himself, then Cam, his bestie, had noticed Charlie sitting outside and dared him to drop one as close to her as possible, without actually hitting her.

He'd tried to back out of it. Said it wasn't right, that she'd hate it. Get mad. But then they'd started winding him up. Saying he must fancy her or something, and he hadn't needed that rumour starting, so he'd done it. He'd forced a laugh, as if he really hadn't cared, but he had. He'd not wanted to upset her and, as he'd suspected, she'd been furious. Storming inside, soaking wet, the yellow dress she'd been wearing stuck to her, and she'd screamed at him. Called him a whole load of names he wouldn't be comfortable saying in front of Alice.

Inside, he'd felt guilty, but because of Cam and the others he'd toughed it out. Acted as if he weren't bothered.

'I'm really sorry about that. Honestly. I never wanted to make you mad.'

'Well, you did.'

He nodded. 'Want to get even?'

She laughed. 'Strangely enough, I don't have any water balloons handy.'

'You have a garden hose.'

Charlie looked at him, incredulous. 'Don't be ridiculous.'

'I'm not.' He replaced the washer. It had worn through. He quickly reassembled the tap, turned the water back on and ran the tap. It worked perfectly. The water shutting off without a singular drip. 'I mean it.'

She laughed, not quite believing him.

So he decided to make her believe. He made a *watch this* face, then walked out to the back porch door, opened it and strode through into the back garden. He located the tap by the hose and turned it on, handed it to a bewildered Charlie and then stood in the middle of the lawn. Arms wide open, smiling right at her. Daring her. 'Do your worst.'

He was kidding, right? How had trying to fix a tap turned into this? It had been a simple Saturday morning, she'd been getting things done and then she and Alice were going to go for a walk around Vasquez later, to get better acquainted with the town. Maybe pop into the diner, because a patient during the week had told her that they made the most amazing pistachio ice cream and she knew that was one of Alice's favourites.

But then Gayle had offered to send Eli round to fix the tap and, though she'd not been happy about that fact, she'd accepted it. How long would it take, after all? Not long, right? He could be in and out within the hour and her day could carry on as normal.

But now he wanted her to douse him in water?

At the end of the hose was a nozzle that allowed her to alter the water. Spray. Mist. Soak. High Pressure. Low Pressure. She could use any one and clearly he wanted her to do it. Was offering her the chance to get even, but she stood there, hesitating.

'Come on! Get your revenge!' Eli laughed.

He was fully clothed! He was going to get soaked! But she recalled their arrival on the pier and how he'd waded into the bay to fetch her floating suitcase and the way he'd driven her to her new home in soaking-wet clothes. Clearly he didn't worry about things like that.

And there was a small part of her that wanted to get her own back.

She raised the nozzle and pointed it at him.

He smiled back at her, nodded. *Do it.*

Smiling, she reached forward and twisted the nozzle to high pressure—and then let him have it full blast.

Eli gasped as the cold water hit him squarely in

the chest, but he didn't try to run, or to avoid the water stream, he just started to laugh and blow water droplets away from his face as it sprayed upwards, splashing him, and before Charlie knew it she was laughing, too. Laughing so hard she almost couldn't catch her breath. So that her stomach began to hurt and, once he was thoroughly drenched, she dropped the hose to the floor and put her hands on her knees to try and catch her breath.

She became aware that he had stepped close to her and she stood up and one look at his face had her laughing again, until he ran his hands through his long hair to get the wet strands from his face and she felt a punch of lust to the gut. The water was making his jeans and tee and flannel shirt stick to every delicious, muscled inch of him and suddenly it wasn't funny any more.

'Mom, what are you doing?' Alice asked from the back door.

Her head whipped round so fast. 'Nothing, honey. We had a bit of an accident with the hose.'

Alice giggled at the state of Eli.

'You'd better come in. Dry off. I can put your clothes in the dryer.'

'It's okay.'

'No. I can't let you drive around in wet clothes again. This seems to be a theme and I know how it feels, so…' She led him back into the cottage and pointed at the bathroom. 'There are towels in there. Bring your wet clothes when you come back out.'

He left wet footprints across the dark, hardwood floors and she mopped them over with paper towel, until he came back out, bare-chested, with a pink, fluffy towel wrapped around his waist.

His chest was magnificent. Developed pecs that were glorious to look at. Beneath, a six-pack that was enviable. Tight and bristling with muscle.

Huh. I didn't think this through. Or did I?

She felt an eyebrow raise and she couldn't stop herself from taking in every delicious inch of skin. She licked her lips and swallowed hard, smiling as she took his wet pile of clothes from him. 'Couldn't wear the bathrobe on the back of the door, huh?'

He smiled ruefully. 'It didn't fit.'

'Ah. Won't be a minute.' She took his clothes to the dryer room and popped them into the machine, praying that the thirty-minute economy cycle would be the fastest thirty minutes in the history of time. Perhaps she could hide out in the laundry room? It needed a little tidy and there was a pile of clothes there that needed folding. But she could hear Alice's bright voice showing Eli her dragon picture that she'd drawn, and leaving her daughter out there alone with a guy who had nothing on beneath his towel seemed wrong, even though she knew that Eli was a good guy.

'That's amazing, Ally! That fire looks great!'

He was calling her Ally? No one called her Ally. Her name was Alice. 'Let's see.'

Alice showed her the picture and, Charlie had to admit, it was pretty great. There was detail there that she would never have expected a five-year-old to have added—creases around the eyes, scales along the body. There was depth to the picture, so that it wasn't completely two-dimensional. 'Alice, this is amazing! You're so good!'

Alice beamed. 'Thanks. Will you put it on the fridge?'

'Better. I'll get it framed. Hang it on the wall and when you're a rich and famous artist, I'll be able to show people your early work.'

Her daughter chuckled and headed off back to her bedroom to draw some more.

'She's a good kid.'

'She's the best.'

'You're lucky.'

She glanced at him. A quick look was all she could safely manage. Anything longer meant her gaze lingered on his finer details and she didn't want to be focusing on anything like that, thank you very much. His nipples were exposed. That low V from his hipbones was visible. She swallowed hard. 'I am?'

'To have had Alice. To have started a family.'

'Well, you have one, too.'

He nodded. 'I do. And they're great. The best, actually.'

But he sounded sad about something and she couldn't work out why. If they were the best, then what did he have to be sad about? 'Wish they'd found you sooner?'

He met her gaze. Briefly. Before she felt her cheeks flame and she had to turn away. 'Sure.'

Charlie nodded, smiling, straightening the pile of magazines on the coffee table. 'Do you, er... want another drink? We didn't get to drink the last one.'

He straightened a leg, drawing her eye as it tracked his movement. She saw a thick, darkly haired leg and swallowed hard, imagining what it led up to.

'Coffee would be great, thanks.'

Charlie scurried into the kitchen, glad of the escape. She rinsed out the old mugs, washed them, dried them and began making coffee again. It gave her something to do with her hands. Made her feel purposeful. Calmed her. At least until he spoke and she realised he was leaning against the doorjamb in his towel, watching her. 'What made you come to Vasquez?'

She turned guiltily, spilling the milk on the floor. Damn! Why was she so clumsy around him? He was making her nervous. He had no right to make her nervous! 'Oh, you know. I fancied a change. Wanted to get away from the big city.'

'You always loved the city.'

She mopped the milk with paper towels, nodding. 'I did, yes, but sometimes you have too much of a good thing.' She stood again and dropped the paper towels into the trash.

He frowned. 'Can you?'

She glanced at him. A muscled, handsome god. He was the epitome of a good *thang*.

'Oh, yes.'

'What did you have too much of in Anchorage?'

What was this? The Spanish Inquisition? Her cheeks flamed at the thought of all she'd gone through with Glen. The way he'd put their relationship online. The secret videos he'd taken of the two of them, in their bedroom. The photos he'd taken of her without her consent, sharing them with his friends. The embarrassment. The *humiliation*.

Glen had thought it hilarious. Laughing at her when she'd turned up at his door, humiliated and furious. It was why she was so sensitive to being made fun of. It brought it all back and Eli was the champion of practical jokes. He wouldn't understand and nor would she tell him about it, because what if he tried to look her up online? He'd see it all and it was bad enough that her work friends at the last hospital she'd worked at—a place where she'd considered putting down roots for the first time—had seen them, forcing her to move away again. To resist the urge to settle. To keep on running. To keep on moving. Never giving anyone time enough to witness her shame. To know that she would always have to do this, if she was to keep her anonymity.

But Eli changed all of that, because she didn't have anonymity with him. He knew parts of her. They'd lived in the same building for years together and, whether you were close or not, that still allowed someone to know you.

'I don't really want to go into all of that.' She handed him the coffee mug and stepped away, almost as if he were poison. As if he was dangerous. And in a way, he was. It should be illegal to look the way he looked. She knew he worked at it. She'd seen him on that first day and he'd told her that he liked to start the day with a bit of cardio. But he made it look effortless. Easy. And she knew it was anything but. He'd not really been into fitness as a teenager. What had changed? Had he just seen all those guys on social media with six-packs? Or all those superhero movies where the guys were ripped and wanted to look the same? Was it ego?

'Why not? Did something happen?'

'You ask a lot of questions.'

'You avoid answering them.'

'Yes, well, maybe I don't want to share with you.'

He grinned. 'Oh, come now. I'm a good listener. A problem shared is a problem halved, or so they say.'

'Well, *they* say wrong. No amount of sharing will ever solve that issue. In fact *sharing* is what caused the issue in the first place.' The kitchen felt small with his hulking form in it and so she walked past him, irritated, into the living space and sat down, cradling her mug and hoping he'd change the subject.

Eli slowly followed her in and settled down in a chair opposite her. 'You know what I think you need?'

'What?' She sounded petulant and hated it. She didn't want to be so irritated, or snippy, but Eli was creeping very close to the big open wound that she nursed on a daily basis.

'You need to relax.'

'Is that your official diagnosis, Doctor?'

He smiled. 'It is. You seem tense. Stressed. You need to experience the Vasquez beauty and chill out for a little while.'

'And how would I achieve that, exactly?'

'Next weekend. You, me and Alice, if you want, go for a drive up to Lawton Lake. I'll take the paddle boards, we'll have fun and then afterwards the beauty of the place will bring your blood pressure down a few notches. What do you say?'

It sounded amazing. But a whole day with Eli? Having fun? Spending time together deliberately? In a beautiful, secluded spot? Could be dangerous, too. But with Alice there…nothing would happen. So… 'All right. I've never tried paddleboarding. I've always wanted to.'

'Then it's a date.' He smiled.

CHAPTER SEVEN

ELI WOULD DESCRIBE himself as a guy who was comfortable in his own skin. He'd got to know his body quite well over the years, especially during his cancer treatment. He'd had so many scans he was amazed he didn't glow in the dark. And afterwards, when he'd pursued health and fitness? He'd got used to focusing on muscle groups, or improving his cardiovascular system, or taking up yoga to stretch and breathe and focus. He made sure his body was a finely tuned machine and he was proud of it. Felt comfortable in it.

Until he had to wear a solitary towel at Charlie's house and knew he would have to control his thoughts.

Alice was about, for one, even if she was mostly in her room, but as he'd chatted with Charlie in the kitchen and stood close to her a couple of times, he'd felt a definite arousal at being around her and had had to cool his jets.

When she'd sat away from him, he'd taken a little sigh of relief, thanking his lucky stars and praying that the dryer would be finished soon, so he could get dressed, because the thought kept repeating in his head that he was nearly naked with Charlie Griffin and Charlie seemed utterly oblivious to the effect she was having on him.

She was most definitely his type. It was something he'd been aware of back in the orphanage, though he'd been able to hide it in the teasing and the jokes, and it was something he was most definitely aware of now. He'd not meant to ask her out like that. To imply a date of any kind. But she seemed so tense all the time and he knew that if she just sat back for a little while and let the beauty of Vasquez in, then she would feel herself unwinding.

She was wound tight right now. Prickly and unforgiving and he was interested in seeing what she'd be like if she let loose. He always had been.

He'd seen a brief image as she'd sprayed him with that water and collapsed with laughter and it had been in that moment, as the water had gushed at him and she'd been laughing, he'd seen a glimpse of the real Charlie.

And he really liked what he'd seen and wanted more.

Her eyes had sparkled, her mouth wide and her laughter? Her real laugh and not the polite one she used at work when she was humouring him? Oh, dear Lord, that laughter was moreish. He wanted to hear it again and again. He wanted to see her face relax, that broad smile, hear that lovely sound, but more than anything he wanted to be the cause of it. Wanted her to collapse with laughter into his arms and gaze up into his eyes and…

It was the same as when they'd been kids. He'd wanted to make her smile. Wanted to make her laugh, but she'd always seemed to react differently to him joking around and hadn't laughed the way the other kids had. He'd thought maybe the practical-joke route and clowning around weren't the way to her heart, and so he'd backed off for a bit, but then the Clarks had come and he'd been about to leave, and the only way he'd known to say goodbye was to play one last trick…

But he was an adult now and though the urge to revert to type was strong every time he looked at her, he also knew he had to approach her differently.

Charlie was skittish. Someone or something had hurt her and he knew how that felt. But Charlie wore her wound out in the open, whereas he hid his, under layers and layers of smiles and confidence so that something like that would never happen again.

Because he wouldn't allow it.

If you didn't put your trust in people, then they couldn't betray you.

Everyone put their trust in him. He was their doctor. He was a Clark now, and that was fine, because he knew he was dependable and he wanted people to trust him. He just couldn't do it in return, because that was harder and so he remained out in the open, armoured by his sense of humour.

From the utility room, there was a ping and then silence.

'Your clothes are dry!' Charlie got up so fast, he felt a wry smile cross his face, glad that she'd been just as uncomfortable with the situation as he'd been.

When she passed him his clothes they were warm and soft. 'Thanks.'

'I'll leave you to get dressed.' She gave him a smile and closed the door to the utility, so he had privacy.

Eli dropped the towel and put on his jersey shorts, then jeans, then tee, then flannel shirt. She must have put a scented dryer sheet in with the clothes because now he smelled like her, which was a little disturbing and not altogether unpleasant.

He scooped up the towel, folded it and placed it on a wooden rail. When he stepped out of the room, the relief on her face made him smile.

'Well, thank you for fixing the tap, Eli, and coming over so promptly. I appreciate that and I'd hate to take up more of your Saturday.'

'It was no problem. I guess I'll see you Monday?'

She nodded. 'You will.'

He grabbed his bag of tools from the kitchen. 'Say goodbye to Alice for me.'

'Of course.' She opened the front door and stood there expectantly, hoping, clearly, that he would just walk straight out and disappear.

But the urge to mess with her mind one last time surged forth in his brain. Having intently watched her deal with his inherent nakedness and the fact that he'd asked her and Alice to go paddle-boarding with him, he knew he couldn't just walk out.

He stopped right beside her, as he went to go. Smiled and then bent forward to kiss her on the cheek.

He hoped to see her cheeks flame with colour. They did.

He hoped she'd look a little awkward and not know where to look. She did.

He thought it would make him smile.

But brushing his lips over her soft, soft skin and inhaling the scent of her did strange things to his own insides, muddling his thoughts and confusing him, and it was almost as if he couldn't get his mouth to form the word goodbye.

All he could manage was a nod and then he was stepping out into the clean Vasquez air and away towards his truck.

As he got behind the wheel, he was still mulling over how it had felt to kiss her.

But more importantly, he was disturbed by the urge he'd had to press his lips to hers and kiss her as she'd never been kissed before.

CHAPTER EIGHT

'I CAN'T TELL you how nice it is to have a lady doc back again,' said Teresa Muller, who sat in front of Charlie in her own consultation room. Her time shadowing Eli was over and she was familiar with the layout of this place and how Eli liked things done. 'I love Eli to bits, but sometimes you just like to talk to another girl, you know?'

Charlie nodded. 'And what can I do for you today?'

Teresa sighed. 'Well, I think I'm at that age in which I might need a little something-something.'

Teresa was fifty-one. 'What exactly do you need me to help you with?'

'Hormones! That replacement stuff.' Teresa leaned in and whispered, 'I think I'm in meno-pause.'

'Okay. What have your symptoms been?'

'Where do I begin? I get those hot-flash things. Feel like someone's turned the heating way up high in the middle of my chest. It creeps up my neck, makes me go bright red, I begin to sweat like I'm in a sauna.' Teresa leaned in again. 'I'm no oil painting to begin with, but when one of those things begins, I look and feel awful! Don't do my marriage no favours, let me tell you, and that's the other thing.' She began to whisper again. 'It's gone funny. *Down there.*'

'You're experiencing dryness?'

'Damn straight! Makes no sense, when I've got so much water pouring out of my head and down my back, that down there is drier than the Sahara. It hurts when we…you know! And my Greg, he's a patient, understanding man, but I've had to tell him to stop so many times, because it hurts, he's started not even trying to initiate… well…you know.'

'Have you tried lubrication?'

'I ordered some online and it does help, but it takes the romance out of it, when you have to stop to use it first, you know? I'm hoping those replacement hormones might give me back some of my go-go juice, if you'll pardon the expression.'

Charlie smiled. 'Any other symptoms?'

'Does a bear poop in the woods? I'm tired. My body aches. Sometimes I can't remember anything anyone's told me. I get headaches. Ratty. That's the other thing. My Greg says I can go from happy and smiley to grizzly bear in an instant!'

'So you've noticed a change in your mood?'

Teresa nodded. 'I have and he's right. I just

want to be *myself* again, Charlie. I can't remember what it's like to just be me. To just live and not worry. It's just… I feel like I'm losing myself and that's a scary thing. Becoming someone you don't recognise.'

Charlie could understand. She'd like to just live and be the woman she was before Glen ruined her life. Since the humiliation of Glen putting all that stuff out there on the Internet and she'd practically gone into hiding, she didn't like who she'd become, either. She'd always been a little bit twitchy, but since the disaster with him, it had got worse.

She did some basic observations on Mrs Muller, checking her blood pressure, her height, her weight. She read up on her patient's history and saw there was no family history of blood clots, breast cancer or strokes. 'You'll need to check your breasts monthly and make sure you attend all your mammogram appointments. HRT is safe, but some cancers respond to the hormones, so you need to be vigilant. Keep using the lubrication, but this should kick in soon and begin to help in that direction. We'll start you on a low dose and see how you go. Come and see me again in three months and we'll reassess. See if we need to raise it, or if it's causing any problems.'

'Thanks, Charlie. You're an absolute doll. What do you think of Vasquez? Beautiful, huh?'

She nodded. 'It most certainly is.'

'You staying long, or...?'

'I'm just covering Nance's maternity leave.'

'Well, I like you. I think you're very nice and you've been very helpful, too. I hope we can make you stay. You never know!' Teresa stood, grinning, and walked to the door.

'You never know,' she agreed. Hiding in Vasquez for the rest of her life. How would that look? How would that feel? Was it even a possibility, with Eli here?' Probably not. Nance would come back eventually, right? And then she wouldn't have a job and this was such a small town, there weren't any other medical facilities she could work at.

The likelihood was she would be moving on from here at the end of her contract. Not back to Anchorage, though. She couldn't face people there. It would just be tricky. So somewhere else, then. But where? It would all depend on what job opportunities there were.

She had no more patients waiting after Teresa Muller. So she typed up her notes, cleaned down her room and decided she'd go make herself a coffee. See if anyone else had any interesting cases.

As she passed Eli's consulting room, she could hear his voice and she stopped when she heard him laugh out loud.

Her tummy was doing strange things as she lingered by his door, remembering yesterday when he'd seemed to linger slightly after dropping that kiss on her cheek when he'd said good-bye. Her tummy had done strange things then, too. She'd not known where to look. She certainly hadn't been able to meet his eyes, but then he'd been striding away from her, down the path, towards his truck and she'd been mesmerised by the way the wind caught his long hair, the way he moved, the way his eyes briefly met hers before he got inside his vehicle.

It had been like a lightning strike.

Had he really just been practically naked in her home for half an hour?

How on earth did I get through that?

Charlie was so lost in her reverie, she didn't notice that the voices inside the room had changed from conversational to ones of people saying goodbye and suddenly the door to Eli's room was opening and, because she'd been leaning against it, listening, lost in her thoughts, she practically stumbled in.

'Oh! Sorry, I was…er…' Her brain scrambled for an excuse as Eli and a silver-haired old gentleman stared at her quizzically and with wry amusement, as if they knew *exactly* what she'd been doing. 'I was just about to knock.'

There. That seems believable, right?

'Oh? You need me for something?' Eli asked.

He came to stand by her as his patient doffed his cap at her and said, 'Good morning, miss.'

After the patient had gone, Charlie quickly

realised that her mouth wasn't going to work properly, especially as her brain seemed to have stopped functioning. 'Yes, um…it's about next weekend. I don't think I'm going to be able to make it.'

'Oh.'

He looked disappointed, which made her feel… what?

'Yeah, it's just what with Alice being in school now and everything, I don't get to see her and spend time with her as often as I'd like and the weekends are usually our special time and…'

She could see that he was smiling again, almost as if he was tolerating her. That he could see she was using Alice as an excuse. Her voice trailed off. 'Why are you smiling?'

'You're freaking out because I said it's a date. I didn't mean it as a *date* date. Like romance and asking you out. I meant it as *Okay, we've agreed to go paddle-boarding.* I swear to you, I'm not going to try to seduce you.'

'Good. I'm glad, because you would have failed,' she said, feeling a little disappointed that he could so easily dismiss the idea of being on a date with her. That maybe she'd been wrong to imagine all the things she'd imagined, but she always had had a very active imagination.

'If I was going to seduce you, I would have done it yesterday, when I wasn't wearing anything but a towel,' he said seductively, moving closer to her, causing her to take a step back as her cheeks flamed.

She smiled nervously. Wanting to back further away, but the doorjamb was in the way and she collided with it awkwardly. Her brain flooded with the images of him from the weekend. Chest bare. Strong arms on show. His powerful legs and that pink, fluffy towel wrapped tightly around his waist. How his mere physical presence had felt, so close to her in her own home.

Had he meant, just now, to remind her of that moment? Knowing that she would remember how he looked, just to make her blush? Had he mentioned seduction to make her imagine how he might do it? Had he stepped closer to her to see if she would step back?

Was all this just another joke to him? A wind-up? Because that wasn't fair!

'That's good to know,' she managed to say, but her voice didn't sound like her own, it sounded strangled, as if her throat were closing up. His proximity doing alarming things to her blood pressure and pulse rate. And had it got hot in here? Had the air conditioning broken down, somehow?

And then he smiled and stepped away again, as if pleased that he'd had the reaction he'd wanted from her, pleased that she'd amused him, and she didn't like feeling as though she was a plaything. 'I'll take Alice paddle-boarding by myself, if you don't mind,' she said, trying to control the rising anger in her.

'All right.'

Oh. She'd expected him to put up more of a fight. When he didn't, she felt a little deflated.

He'd been testing a theory. Needing to know how she'd react, whether she was as affected by him as he was affected by her.

There was something between them and it wasn't just their shared history. There was something more and he could feel it. It was palpable whenever they were close, or in the same room, especially. It had been there for him when they were kids, but it hadn't been as powerful then, it had just been a crush thing that he'd felt he had to deal with and then forget about when he'd moved away to Vasquez, adopted by the Clarks.

He'd never forgotten Charlie. How could he? She'd been the first girl he'd ever wanted. She was always going to be a piece of his history and that was where he'd relegated her memory.

To history.

But now she was here and, though he knew he had nothing to offer her in the future—she'd always mentioned wanting a large family of her own and he couldn't give her that—he was still sorely tempted by her. One moment he'd be telling himself to just leave it alone. Let her work out her contract and go. But then later, another voice would kick in and tell him to pursue something with her. Let her know in no uncertain terms that what he was offering was temporary but that they both could have some fun, until it was time to leave. Sweeten the history between them.

And so when she'd practically fallen into his office, as if she'd been eavesdropping at the door, he'd wondered why she'd been there. Was she intrigued by him, as attracted to him as he was to her? He'd just had to know, and seeing the look of embarrassment and the way her cheeks had flamed and how fast her pulse had been throbbing at her throat had told him that he was onto something for sure.

He'd kept himself restrained at the weekend, because of Alice's presence, but when they were alone…? That was different.

The only question was…would Charlie want something with no strings attached? Was she that type of person? Or was she so tightly strung, as she appeared to be, that she wouldn't be able to cut loose with him for a while?

He didn't want to use her. He wanted her to get as much out of their short time together as he would. He thought they'd be a great fit together and he knew he would treat her with respect and that somehow, at the end, they would go for a drink and clink their glasses together and toast what fun they'd had. Knew how they'd hug each other and say goodbye on the pier before she flew off with Chuck to go back to the big city.

And then he paused, thinking hard.

Saying goodbye…the thought made him still. Could he lose her for a second time? Would he be able to watch her walk away?

He'd be able to do it. Wouldn't he? He could put whatever they had in a box and push it to one side. He'd have to.

'But it was very kind of you to offer.'

He looked up at her and smiled, nodding.

'I have another offer for you.'

She looked wary. 'Oh?'

'Come on in. Take a seat. You might want to close that door,' he said with a grin, feeling his heart race madly, knowing that if he asked and she said no, then this whole thing was going to be mighty embarrassing. But what did he have to lose?

CHAPTER NINE

SHE WATCHED HIM walk behind his desk and sit down, so after she'd apprehensively closed the door, wondering what this was all about, she did the same, sitting opposite.

Eli gave her an appraising look, a broad smile across his face. 'I think we should get married.'

Charlie stared at him and went still. She didn't blink. She didn't breathe. But internally, her heart raced, her blood pressure went up and adrenaline and cortisol flooded her body. *'What?'*

'I think we should get married,' he said again, watching her intently with amusement.

'This is one of your jokes again, isn't it?' She laughed wryly, but without humour. 'Typical Eli. Always out for a laugh. Well, I don't need it.' She got up out of her chair, glad to see that her legs were still working after that initial shock.

'Okay, okay!' He laughed. 'That was a joke. I couldn't help it, you looked so...tense.'

'I wonder why?' she said, heart still thudding.

'I apologise. Do you forgive me?'

He looked at her with such sweet, imploring eyes, she felt her anger begin to fade. Part of her did not want to forgive him at all! But another, more logical part knew that she still had to work with him for a while longer and work would be a whole lot easier if they were getting along. 'Fine. But only if you're going to be serious.'

'Life's too short for serious. You have to have fun sometimes.'

'Do you really have something you want to talk to me about?'

He nodded. 'I do.'

'Well, get on with it, then! The clinic could be filling with patients.'

He tapped a couple of keys on his keyboard, then turned his screen so she could see. Apparently Eli could access the security cameras in the waiting room. And the waiting room itself? Was empty. There was no way she could leave by saying she had a patient waiting.

'What do you want to talk to me about, Eli?'

'I do want to talk about us, that bit is true.'

Us.

What did he want? Was he going to probe into their pasts? Talk some more about what it had been like together as kids? Or was he going to talk about her being here? That there didn't seem to be enough work for two people sometimes and that maybe he'd made a mistake in asking her here? And that last unexpected thought suddenly terrified her. Because, as much as she hated knowing that Eli knew about her past, the idea of leaving Vasquez was scary. Probably because Alice was settling so well into kindergarten and was loving every minute of Mrs Clark's classes. Probably because she had nothing else in the pipeline just yet. Probably it was because, despite the overfamiliarity of the residents of Vasquez, she had never felt so welcomed anywhere. Probably it was because when she lay in bed alone at night, she harboured secret thoughts of what it might be like to actually settle here.

'Us?'

'Yes. I like you, Charlie, and I think you like me, too.' He smiled, waiting for her response.

'You're not too bad, I guess.'

'I don't mean as friends.'

'You mean as…work colleagues?'

'No. I do not. I mean I think I want to talk about the fact that we're both attracted to one another.' He was searching her face, looking for clues that she agreed with him.

He was right. She was attracted to him. But she didn't normally just come straight out and tell a guy that. She usually let them buy her a drink. Take her out on dates. It was something done gradually. Incrementally. Each date either increasing or decreasing that attraction until it reached critical level and they either fell into bed with one another or split up. Or she moved away.

She never just admitted it out loud.

It felt weird.

'Well, that's the elephant in the room,' she said, not sure what else to say.

'I thought it best to acknowledge it. I'm a straightforward guy.'

'Are you saying this because you mean it? Or are you saying this because you can't actually go out with anyone in Vasquez, because, technically, they're all your patients and that would be stepping over a line?'

He got up out of his chair and came to stand by her. Looking down at her. Intensity in his eyes.

His proximity caused her heart to race again.

'Because I mean it and I think we're two responsible adults, who both have a bit of freedom, who could maybe take advantage of that attraction.'

She stood up to face him, not liking how it felt to have him tower over her like that. She wanted to feel stronger. More assured. Even though her mouth had gone dry and her palms had gone sweaty. 'I thought you said you weren't trying to seduce me,' she whispered.

'I'm not. I'm talking about us both using the time we have together to enjoy a bit of…adult fun. No strings attached. No life getting in the way and when it's over, it's over. We part as friends and with some pretty excellent memories of the time we shared together.'

'You're talking about a fling?'

He took another step closer. His gaze drifting down towards her lips as he smiled 'I'm talking about a fling. So, Charlie Griffin. What do you say to my…proposal?'

She should slap him across the face. Maybe accuse him of sexual harassment? And if she did then he would profusely apologise and make sure he scheduled their work so she didn't have to be there at the same time as him, if that would make her day and time here easier.

He was prepared for both.

But she did neither. For a while, she just stared at him and he could tell her mind was racing with possibilities. Possible actions. Possible responses.

She was fighting an internal battle and he wondered which side would win. The side that just wanted to work out her contract and get away from Vasquez as quickly as she'd arrived? Or the side that was attracted to him and wondered what it might be like if she was brave enough to take this further?

'This…fling…it would be private between us?' Her cheeks had reddened.

'It would. Unless you wanted otherwise.'

'You wouldn't worry about people finding out?'

'I have nothing to hide. Would you be worried about people finding out?'

She blinked. 'Alice. I don't want there to be a string of men in her mother's life that she has to call Uncle.'

So she was seriously contemplating this.

'And this isn't a joke?' she asked.

'Maybe I could prove it?'

'How?'

'By kissing you. And then you could tell me afterwards, if I truly meant it. If it felt real. And if you had any doubts about my intent afterwards, you could end it as quickly as it began.'

She blushed and looked away. 'A kiss?'

'One kiss.' He stepped closer, desperate to touch her. Desperate to stroke her cheek with his finger. To run his hands into her hair. To hold her against him. 'A fair test, wouldn't you say?'

'I could say a lot of things.'

'Charlie?'

'What?'

'Say yes. To a single. Solitary. Mind-blowing kiss.' His voice had grown husky as his desire for her increased.

She looked up at him, deeply into his eyes, searching for something. To see if he was still, somehow, joking? To make sure he was serious? But there was something else there.

Desire.

Charlie wanted this—he could tell. She was just trying to work out how to give herself permission.

Her hand suddenly rose and she pressed it upon his chest and he hoped she could feel how fast his heart was beating for her. Her fingers spread slightly and her hand moved over his pectoral muscle and stilled.

Thump-thump.

Thump-thump.

Her touch made him want to do a thousand things to her. To take her in his arms and push her up against the wall. To rip her blouse out of her waistband and allow his hands to explore her soft flesh. To taste her. To hear her groan with pleasure.

But he'd made a promise. Just a kiss.

One kiss.

A smile hesitantly touched her lips. 'All right. One kiss.'

Triumphant, he slowly began to lean in.

The smile broadened. 'Let's see what you can do,' she whispered.

Eli grinned. 'Challenge accepted.'

And he slowly pressed his lips to hers.

CHAPTER TEN

IT WAS ALL just going to be pretty wrapping. Wasn't it? That was what she told herself before the kiss. That all the muscles, the tattoos, the long, dark brown, Viking-esque hair, the smile, the twinkle in the eyes, were all dressing and that maybe, once she kissed him, she would be able to relax and realise that that was all it was. Because there wouldn't be any depth. There wouldn't be any *feelings* and once it was proved, once and for all, she'd be able to put this irritating attraction that she had for Eli to bed.

But she was wrong.

So *incredibly* wrong.

It wasn't just aesthetics. It wasn't that he was just so tall, and so broad and so strong. His lips touched hers, so softly at first. Tenderly. Tentatively. A whisper of his lips against hers. A brush that promised a heat. An awakening of the senses.

And then it all changed.

Everything. Dizzying. All at once. An overwhelming feeling as his tongue passed by her lips and entered her mouth, and the knowledge that he had penetrated her somehow, that she had allowed him access because she wanted it, seemed to stir something within her as the kiss deepened.

Her hands came to rest against his chest, without her realising, as the rest of the world dropped away and all that seemed to matter was the two of them, pressed against one another as she tasted him. Feeling the brush of his light beard against her skin. Inhaling the scent of him, her senses going into overdrive, every nerve ending alive and expectant of more.

And as she sank into him, as she allowed herself to enjoy and experience his kiss, to yearn for more, to yearn to feel his flesh beneath her fingertips, he pulled back and away and stared at her, smiling. Leaving her breathless. Wanting more. Why had he stopped? Was this another joke?

No…it wasn't a joke. His eyes were dark with desire.

The attraction was real and she wanted him.

And he was offering himself to her if she wanted it.

No strings attached, he'd said.

She felt stunned by his kiss. A little wild inside as if she wanted to lock the door behind him, sweep everything off his desk and have wild and crazy sex with him, right there, in that very room.

His offer would allow her to sate her desires

and then leave again, with no complications, because there'd be no way she was going to fall for Eli. This was lust, pure and simple, right? It was all it could be. But she'd allowed herself to trust a guy before and her instincts had been wrong. He'd secretly filmed her. Had hidden cameras. Had put that stuff on the Internet and Alice might grow up and one day see it. She didn't think she had the misfortune of running into two guys exactly the same. She didn't think Eli would have cameras anywhere, but…this was his office and maybe she could have what she wanted, without putting herself at risk?

'That was a good kiss.'

His smile increased. 'I'm glad.'

'But this is our workplace and we can't do anything here.'

'We just did. Look, come paddle-boarding with me. Come up to Lawton Lake. It's quiet up there. Isolated. We could have some time alone.'

'What about Alice?'

'I can behave myself around your daughter. But I'd like to spend time with you, even if I can't touch you.'

She frowned. 'It's that easy?'

'Stopping myself from touching you? No.' He reached up to stroke her face, had another thought and pulled her close once again, more forceful this time, as if knowing his moments with her would have to be brief.

She sank into the kiss once again, amazed once again as to how the world fell away, all her cares disappearing. Moaning softly, her desire rocketing high, she reached to pull up his shirt, needing to feel his flesh beneath her fingertips, when suddenly, there was a knock at his door and someone was opening it and they broke apart so quickly. Guiltily.

Dot, the receptionist, put her head around the door.

Had she seen? Did she know what they'd been doing?

But Dot's face remained normal. 'Eli? Printer's playing up again. Can you come and give it your magic touch?'

Eli nodded. 'Of course!' He passed Charlie by and she pressed her fingertips to her lips, before smiling at Dot.

'Tech problems?'

'Always. But Eli can fix anything.' Dot looked her up and down. 'And anyone.' She smiled.

The rest of the week passed in a blur. Charlie worked hard and saw a wide variety of patients. A young child who had hurt their hand after grabbing an iron that was cooling down. A case of pneumonia. A spider bite that had become infected. She was enjoying herself immensely here in Vasquez—the range of health queries and injuries that came through their doors at the clinic

was wide and varied, from the normal and every-
day to the crazy, like the guy who came in after
he'd actually tried to juggle a chainsaw and the
even younger guy who'd climbed a tree, slipped
and fallen through the branches, impaling himself on a stick. Her eyes had nearly dropped out
of her head when he'd come walking in through
the sliding doors, half a branch sticking out of
his abdomen, smiling self-consciously. The kid
had been lucky. The branch hadn't gone through
any of his major organs, but rather than remove
the branch themselves, in case it was blocking
any major bleeders, they had stabilised him and
flown him out to a major hospital.

It was strange working in the same building as
Eli, passing him in the corridors, sharing a secret
smile with him around the other staff. Occasionally their hands would brush as they passed each
other in the corridor and every single time her
body lit up like a fourth of July parade. Once,
he'd even pulled her into a linen cupboard, just
to kiss her, and when they'd both emerged... It
was fair to say they'd both looked a little ruffled.
The anticipation of their snatched moments was
adrenaline-fuelled. Hiding. Trying to act normal
around everyone else.

Her dreams at night filled with him and what it
might be like to actually *be* with him. Physically.
Her dreams had become so erotic at one point,
she'd woken up so aroused that she'd had to take

a very long and very cold shower before she could drop Alice off at school and then go into work.

Mrs Clark greeted her every morning that she dropped Alice off and Charlie would smile and feel awkward that her daughter's teacher had no idea about all the sinful and naughty thoughts she was having about her adopted son.

But all the stolen glances, all the thoughts, all the yearnings...they were all adding up into something quite exciting and, though Charlie was still scared, she'd not had this much fun in ages. Because she knew it wasn't just aesthetics any more.

He looked good.

He tasted good.

His kisses and his touch were amazing.

She could only hope and imagine that the rest was just as mind-blowing.

The weekend came around quickly and the day that she would be going up to Lawton Lake with him. She woke, her body fizzing with nerves, her hands trembling with so much anticipation she dropped her tube of toothpaste in the sink and she could barely floss her teeth.

But when she went to wake up Alice, her daughter looked pale and ill.

'Mommy, I don't feel well.'

Instantly, her nerves dissipated as a new concern entered her brain and took prime position. 'What's wrong?'

'My tummy hurts.'

Lots of kids got tummy aches. This was probably nothing. But if Alice was ill, they couldn't go out today. It was her first time being in kindergarten and she was being exposed to a whole new plethora of germs and bacteria, it was no wonder she was ill.

I should have expected this.

'Do you feel sick?'

A nod.

'Okay, honey. Well, we won't go out today, then. Don't you worry about that.'

'I wanted to go paddle-boarding with Eli.'

'So did I. But that lake won't disappear and maybe we could do it next weekend? I'll call Eli and let him know, you just rest. Here.' She passed her daughter her tablet. 'Why don't you watch some cartoons? Take your mind off it. I'll go get you a drink and some dry toast, in case you want to try and eat.'

She felt disappointed, yet also somehow relieved. Charlie had wanted Eli, yes, but the last time she'd fallen for a guy, he'd turned out to be wholly unreliable and weird and, though Eli was nothing like the last one, there had still been that fear that she was rushing into something again, just because of an infatuation. And doubt was an insidious drug, too. Maybe starting something with, not only her work colleague, but her boss was a dangerous thing?

Maybe this was life telling her that this thing with Eli shouldn't get off the ground at all? That they'd had their fun. They'd shared spectacular kisses and fumbles in closets and that would have to be enough.

Downstairs, she picked up her phone and rang him.

He answered straight away. 'Hi.'

'Hey, Eli, listen, I'm sorry, but we won't be able to make it today.'

'Oh.' He sounded incredibly disappointed. 'Are you having second thoughts?'

'No.' She smiled, even though it was partly a lie. 'But I do have an ill Alice. She's woken up with a bad tummy and feels sick. I guess I should have expected something like this, what with her having started school, but I need to stay here and look after her.'

'Of course. Do you need anything?'

'No, no. We're fine. I'm sorry we've had to put off our weekend.'

'Well, the lake isn't going anywhere, so maybe another time?'

She smiled. She'd said the exact same thing to her daughter. 'Absolutely, unless...'

'Unless what?'

'Unless this is a sign that maybe we shouldn't be doing it at all?'

'You believe in signs?'

She shrugged. 'I don't know. Maybe?'

'Okay. Well, is it a sign that you want to follow?'

She thought of him. Of his kisses. His lips. His tongue.

Dear God, his tongue...

Of the way he made her feel all excited and that everything had possibilities. That she wanted to feel that way again. 'No.'

There was a silent pause. 'Good. I'm glad. Want me to come round? I could sit with you. Help you take care of her.'

'I don't know if that's a good idea.'

'I can help. And I promise to control myself in front of your daughter.'

She liked that he was offering to help. And this way? She could still see him. 'Okay.' She smiled.

CHAPTER ELEVEN

HE CALLED IN to the shop first. Bought ice lollies, jelly and some plain dry crackers for Alice. Then he picked up some items for himself and Charlie. They might not be able to go to Lawton Lake, but he was still determined that they would have a good day together.

When he arrived at her door, she opened it with a smile and he raised his bag of shopping. 'I've brought supplies.'

'How long do you think you're staying?' she asked with a quiet laugh.

'Long enough for you to be glad I called round.'

She stepped back. 'Come on in.'

He waited for the door to be closed, then he turned to her. 'Where's Alice?'

'In her room. Sleeping.'

'She okay?'

'It's just a virus, or something.'

He smiled and stepped towards her. Bent his head towards her to let her know he was coming in for a kiss, now that he'd clarified the fact that Alice wouldn't see.

The smile on her face was enough for him to know that his kiss was welcome and he pressed his lips to hers. She let out a small groan in her throat that did all kinds of exciting things to his insides, that told him she'd been looking forward to this.

Because so had he. The thoughts of spending this Saturday with her at Lawton Lake had been all he could think about. He'd imagined getting them both on their paddle boards, teaching them how to balance. How to get back on their board when out on the water, if they fell in. The water at the lake was notoriously calm. Flat. It was the perfect place for them to learn and the scenery around it, breathtaking. But he'd known he wouldn't need to look around to have his breath stolen away. Being with Charlie would do that and so he didn't need to be at a lake. He didn't need to be in a secluded place with her. He just needed her to be close by. And now...? With her lips pressed to his and her body sinking against his...?

When the kiss ended, she was smiling, which made him smile, too.

'Want a drink?'

'You do make me thirsty,' he said.

She laughed. 'Come through to the kitchen. You can show me what you've got.'

'I could show you right here.'

'The bag, silly! You've been to the shop?'

He growled. He'd known exactly what she'd meant, but he hadn't been able to resist. Following her through to the kitchen, he laid the bag on the counter and got out all the goodies he'd bought. Alice's supplies, a rosé wine, cheeses and meats for a charcuterie board, baguettes, fruit, chips, ice cream.

A huge teddy bear.

'Wow.'

'I thought we could have a picnic in the back yard.'

'Great idea. Coffee?'

'Sure.'

She set about making them both a drink and he watched her move about the kitchen. Now that they had a new understanding between them, he felt able to openly watch her and concentrate on her. There were no other eyes watching them. No one making assumptions. Their fling, their relationship, whatever you wanted to call it, was theirs alone. And she was beautiful to watch. His. He liked that.

While the coffee machine did its thing, he reached out for her hand, taking her fingers in his and pulling her close, up against his body. She looked up at him, mildly amused, her eyes sparkling with mischief. 'Something I can do for you?'

'Plenty of things.'

'Such as?'

He smirked. 'Don't poke the bear, Charlie. Not with your daughter just in the next room. I've woken from hibernation and I want to feed. I want to feed a lot and you just happen to be the snack I want to feast on.'

'Tell me what you want to do to me, then,' she said, teasingly, smiling, looking up at him through thick, lush lashes, her lips parted, the glimpse of her tongue, wet and slick, giving him all sorts of X-rated ideas.

He groaned softly. 'I want to know we have a space that is just our own. No interruptions. Nothing else to worry about but each other's pleasure.' He stroked her cheek with the back of his finger. 'I want to be able to slowly undress you and marvel at every inch of your skin. Touch every inch. Your beautiful neck. This collarbone.' His finger trailed down the slope of her throat, brushing aside her top to reveal her clavicle. 'I want to reveal every delicious part of you. Slowly. Admire you. Kiss you. Taste you.'

He could see her breathing was increasing. Felt her push herself against him.

'I want to take my time over you. Discover what makes you breathe hard. What makes you gasp. What makes you arch your back. What makes you move against me as you beg for more. As you beg me not to stop.' He dropped a soft kiss on her collarbone, inhaled her dreamy scent and then backed off, remembering his promise. Remembering that they weren't alone. That her daughter was in the next room and that no matter how much he wanted to take this further, he could not. He sucked in a deep breath. It wasn't easy moving away from her. Not when he wanted her so badly. It was taking an enormous amount of control, especially since he'd been waiting for this weekend so badly.

She looked disappointed that he moved away, but understanding too. And he saw that she respected him for controlling himself. Charlie cleared her throat. 'Okay. Well, I look forward to us finding a place that's just our own.'

He nodded and smiled. 'Can I go see her? Say hello?'

'Sure.'

They both needed the distraction. They both needed to remember the priority here. It was Alice. Not what they wanted physically. And he didn't want Charlie to think that he was only with her because he hungered for her body. He liked her. Really liked her. Always had. But Charlie had a daughter now and he liked Alice too. She was a great kid.

He knocked on her bedroom door.

'Come in.'

Grinning broadly and holding the huge teddy

bear he'd bought, he poked his head around the door. 'Hi. How you doing? Your mum tells me you're not feeling too great.'

Alice's eyes landed on the bear and widened as she sat up in bed. 'Is that for me?'

'Sure is. A friend for Mr Cuddles.' He passed the bear over and smiled as she hugged it tight. He remembered being her age. Young and in care already, he'd always had dreams of someone turning up one day, maybe on his birthday, with a big bear and a load of gifts that were just for him, that let him know that there was someone out there who cared. That maybe his life so far had been a terrible mistake and they'd not meant to leave him at a fire station when he was a baby. That someone would come and rescue him and let him know that actually he was a prince from a far-off country.

Of course, it never happened. He never got gifts and so he started making his own fun. It was the only way to brighten his day and try to make him forget how lonely and alone he actually was.

Luckily Alice didn't have to experience any of that. She had a mom. She wasn't in a kids' home and she was loved very much. And looking around her room, he saw she had plenty of stuff. Toys, plushies, games, books. He wondered if Charlie had ever felt the same way, too.

'What's his name?' Alice asked.

'I don't know. I think maybe you ought to name him.'

Alice turned the bear to look at his face properly. 'He looks like a Sprinkles.'

Eli grinned. 'Great name! Sprinkles it is.' He looked around her room. Saw her sketch pad on the table. 'You been drawing?'

She nodded.

'Can I take a look?'

Another nod.

He picked up her pad and began to flick through the pages. There was the usual stuff. Cats. Dogs. A unicorn that had been coloured in with a multitude of bright, rainbow colours. And then he came across a drawing that made him smile even more. 'Is that *me*?'

Alice had drawn a picture that was clearly herself, her mom, and a seaplane floating on water, with a man wading through water to reach a case. She'd drawn him big, as if he was a giant, with masses of long, wild hair, and he had a huge smile on his face. He liked it very much.

'Do you like it? You can keep it, if you want.'

He thanked her. 'All great artists *sell* their work. They don't just give it away. I tell you what—I'll give you five dollars so I can put it on my fridge.' He reached into his pocket and pulled a note from his wallet and placed it on her bedside table.

'Mom! Eli gave me five dollars for my drawing!'

Behind him, Charlie walked across the room from her position in the doorway and ruffled her daughter's hair, before laying a hand on her forehead to test her temperature. 'I heard! That's great! You should put it in your little safe and when you're better you can spend it on something nice.'

'I'm already feeling better.'

'You feel it. No temperature. Why don't you go out in the garden and get some fresh air for a bit?'

'Okay.' Alice swung her legs out of bed and grabbed her bathrobe, slid her feet into slippers shaped like bunnies and headed on out.

Charlie turned to look at him. 'That was very sweet. You didn't have to pay her for her drawing.'

'I believe in nurturing talent and she's got one.'

'She's five.'

'And already drawing like a twelve-year-old. Who knows where she'll be in a few years' time?'

He wouldn't know. Because she and Charlie would be leaving in a few months' time. It was painful to think about. Sad.

'Maybe you can call me one day and tell me? I'd like to know how she's doing.'

The idea that they wouldn't be around…that he wouldn't…was sobering.

'You don't have to do that, you know.'

'Do what?'

'Show an interest in my kid because you're interested in me.'

'I'm not. I like Alice and I can tell she's something special.' He frowned. 'You never drew. Who does she get that creativity from? Her father?'

Instantly, he saw the walls come up as her hackles raised. Clearly the father was a difficult subject.

'Glen would consider himself an artist, sure. But I didn't like what he created. What he chose to share with the world.'

He wasn't sure what she meant. 'Was it like, abstract? Weird stuff?'

'He experimented with film.'

'Okay. Would I have seen any of it, anywhere? Did he exhibit?' He got the feeling she was trying to tell him the truth, but felt unable to give concrete details, so she was skirting around the edges of the confession.

'Unfortunately.' She walked past him, towards the kitchen.

He followed her from the room and went to stand beside her as they watched Alice in the garden. Her daughter was sitting by a flower bed, watching something crawl over the back of her hand. A ladybug?

'Why did you break up with this… Glen?' He was curious. He really wanted to know. The Charlie he'd known had been keen to find and create her own family. She'd wanted loads of kids—had said she wouldn't be happy until she had loads of them and would surround herself with their love. That she would create a happy home, with a white picket fence.

'I don't really want to talk about him, if you don't mind?'

'Sure. Sure.' He gazed out of the window, trying not to look at her, but he'd heard something in her voice, just then. A hurt. A pain. A deep wound that she would prefer to ignore, but Eli knew, from practice, that hiding pain only caused it to get worse and fester.

He'd hid his own. Not wanting to tell anyone. Not wanting to tell his brand-new family that he thought something was wrong with him, in case they realised they'd made a bad choice in choosing him, and when he'd got so scared that he'd finally spoken up, it had been far too late. The cancer had been well established and, though the seminoma and his left testicle had been removed, he'd still had to undergo chemotherapy and radiation, which had left him sterile. Since then, he'd thankfully had no recurrences, but he maintained his body as if it was the most precious possession he had on this earth, which of course it was, because the one thing he'd always wanted—a child—would never be within his reach.

'But I'm here for you, if you ever want to.'

He felt, rather than saw, her look over at him, then glance away, before her fingers gently entwined with his, squeezing his hand briefly, before letting go as Alice stood up and came back towards the house.

'Mom, could I have a drink?'

'Sure, though Eli brought some popsicles—want one of those instead?'

'What flavour?'

'Orange or cherry?'

'Orange, please!'

He was glad Alice was okay, though she still had a strange pallor that told him that, whatever she had, she wasn't over it yet.

Alice sat in the living area, holding Sprinkles and sucking on her popsicle and then the television was put on.

Eli leaned against the kitchen counter as Charlie put away the things he'd brought from the shop. When she'd got nothing left to fiddle with, nothing left to clear up, she looked at him awkwardly. 'I bet this is the sexiest fling you've ever had,' she said quietly, so Alice couldn't hear.

He laughed. 'You have no idea.' The truth was, he'd never had a fling with anybody. He'd only ever had serious relationships and none since Lenore. Her leaving had pained him greatly, resulting in him feeling like the best way forward was to never get involved with anyone ever again. Not seriously, anyway.

'If you want to go, you can. I'd hate for you to waste a precious day off, hanging around with us.'

'Forget it! I love hanging around with you guys. You're refreshing.'

'We're new, so we're fun?'

'You're not new to me. I know you, remember?'

'Not deeply, though. You don't know all my deep, dark secrets. You don't know who I've cried over, who I've laughed with, who my friends are, what my favourite food is. You just think you know me because we shared a childhood.'

He considered her, knowing he couldn't let her push him away. He wanted to stay. Wanted to prove to her that she wasn't just a plaything. She was important. 'I know Alice's father hurt you and that you don't want to talk about it. Probably because you're embarrassed about it or ashamed for some reason. I think you've cried over him. Or maybe, more precisely, you've cried over losing what he represented—the happy family unit you always dreamed of having. All those kids. He hurt you, took something from you and you're still healing and you're trying to decide if you can trust a man ever again.

'I think Alice makes you laugh. Alice makes you happy, because it's just you and her against the world and she is your world, because you take her with you everywhere you go. I'd like to think you have loads of friends and maybe you do, but you never stay around long enough for them to know.' He smiled, but not with triumph. 'And your favourite food is grilled cheese. Or at least it was before.'

Charlie stared at him in shock, her face a mask of surprise and fear.

He continued. 'Today, you're a great doctor and I know what it takes to become a doctor in this world, which means that you're clever and strong and determined and you've learned how to harden your heart from all the tragedy and upset in this world, but that in private you still feel it keenly and you shed tears when you're home alone. You're a professional and you want to show your daughter that working is important and that if you want success, you have to earn it. You yearn for relationships, but fear them at the same time. Am I even close?'

He knew it was a scary thing to say all of that, but he had to let her know that he could see the real her and not the shiny exterior that she revealed to their patients. But he also said it all with a grin on his face, because he needed her to know that he wasn't judging her, just trying to show that he knew her better than she realised.

She paused a long while before she answered. 'Maybe you should be a shrink, with insight like that. But are you able to turn that keen eye upon yourself?'

He didn't get a chance to answer because suddenly, from the living area, they heard a strange sound and then Alice was being ill all over the hard wooden floors.

Charlie rushed to her daughter, whereas Eli grabbed paper towels and cleaning spray from under the sink before hurrying over.

Alice was crying. 'I'm sorry, Mom!'

'It's okay, honey. It's okay.'

They cleared her up and took her back to her bedroom, settling her beneath the covers with Sprinkles and giving her her tablet to watch some shows on, a bucket beside her, just in case.

When the drama was over and they were back in the kitchen alone, Eli stared at her. 'I can turn that eye upon myself. I don't get involved in relationships any more because I got hurt so badly in my last one, which was two years ago. I maintain my happy-go-lucky persona because it makes me happy and I like making other people smile. Everyone in Vasquez is my friend, but they are also my patients, so my friendships with them are strange ones. The last time I cried I was twenty-one years of age and I cried because I felt like my happy life I'd built was spinning out of my control. And my favourite food is cheesecake, which is a total bummer, because to look like this?' He indicated his own body with his hands. 'You don't get to eat cheesecake often enough.'

She smiled at him, shyly, clearly pleased that

he'd shared something with her, after he'd so expertly psychoanalysed her. And then she laughed. 'Okay.' She picked a piece of imaginary fluff off the kitchen surface. 'What made you cry?'

His cancer diagnosis. But he didn't want her to know about that. What was the point? It was over with now. Done. He'd had no recurrences and he was too busy living in the present to keep returning to the past. 'I don't remember,' he lied. Hating himself for lying.

'I think you do. You remembered you were twenty-one when it happened, so I also think you do know what caused it, you just don't want to say.'

He crossed his arms and stepped closer to her, towering over her, smiling. 'I tell you what…if you tell me about what happened with Alice's father, I'll tell you why I cried.'

She considered it. He saw it cross her eyes. But then she looked down and away. Defeated. 'I guess we'll never know then, huh?'

Alice slept for a couple of hours and when she woke, she looked much brighter and asked if she could come out and watch a movie with them.

She and Eli had spent the time chatting in the lounge, discussing some of his weirdest cases and sharing tales of their medical training. They'd trained in different schools, but discovered that they'd both done a placement in the same emergency room, though obviously not at the same time, and had shared stories about an attending that they both knew, who'd made an impression on the pair of them with his crazy uncombed hair and the fact that he always sounded as if he was winging his way through the day. Eli had been most amused to hear that this guy had even asked Charlie out once and she'd given him the benefit of the doubt and enjoyed a drink with him, only to put up with the fact that his mother kept texting him all night long and she discovered he lived in her basement. That had been the end of that!

They put on an animated movie and Alice lay between them on the couch. Eli was at Alice's feet and Charlie let her daughter lay her head upon her lap. As the movie played, Eli stretched out his hand across the back of the couch, as if reaching for her fingers, and, once she'd checked that Alice couldn't see, Charlie reached out too.

Their fingers entwined on the back of the couch and Eli looked at her and smiled, his eyes sparkling, and she realised that, even though she'd been worried about Alice and they'd never made it up to Lawton Lake, Eli had still somehow made the day special. He'd not shown boredom once. Had never been impatient. Had never been rude. Never selfish. He'd helped care for Alice. Been thoughtful. He'd been kind and funny and made her laugh and his presence had been reassuring and comforting. He'd made the day easier and she liked having him around. An hour ago, he'd insisted on preparing their charcuterie lunch and had pretended to be her private waiter, pulling out her chair for her to sit down, draping a serviette across her lap and calling her 'miss'.

As she played with his fingers, she wondered about what kind of a father he would make. He seemed to adore kids, so she had no doubt he would make a wonderful dad. Look at how he kept trying to nurture Alice's drawing! That had been so sweet—buying one of her pictures. She'd never seen Alice smile so broadly.

Holding his hand secretly felt good and she found herself smiling and imagining what a future with Eli in her life might look like. And when she realised that she would like it very much, she froze, feeling her heart beat faster.

What am I even thinking?

She risked a glance at him, to see if he'd noticed the change in her, but he hadn't. He was staring at the screen, laughing at the antics of a pack of hyenas.

He might be good with kids because, at heart, he was a kid himself, and hadn't he told her before that he hadn't been in a relationship for over two years? That he'd got hurt and wouldn't risk it again? This was not a man looking for an instant family and nor was she in the market for making one with him.

This was a *fling*.

Or at least was trying to be.

We've only shared kisses. Heated fumbles. Perhaps I should stop this before it goes even further?

CHAPTER TWELVE

'CHARLIE! GREAT—YOU'RE HERE. We've had a field call. Hikers trapped down a crevasse. Mountain Rescue have also been informed, but they've asked for two doctors to attend.'

'Oh, okay. But who will man the clinic?'

'The nurses are here and our resident, has said he'll stay as long as we need him to cover.'

She got up from behind her desk, downing the last of her coffee. 'How are we getting there?'

'Driving most of the way, then I'm afraid it might be a bit of a hike. It's up in the White Mountains.'

She stepped out from behind her desk, to reveal sandal shoes. 'I don't have hiking boots.'

'I think we may have some spares to loan you. We keep a supply, just in case. What size are you?'

'Size nine.'

'Perfect. Come on—I'll talk you through it.' He turned to go, hearing her steps quickly catching up with him as he began to stride down the corridor towards the field supply room. Here they kept everything they would need for a field call. Go bags, filled with equipment they might need—oxygen, defib, masks, gloves, bandages, splints, needles, syringes, painkilling medications. There were jackets and high-vis vests, helmets, boots, torches, blankets, supplies of water, IV bags, a bit of everything and anything. All clearly labelled, so it could just be grabbed quickly.

Eli searched the boots labelled nines and passed a pair to Charlie. 'Try these on. Mountain Rescue will have sent out a team via helicopter, but they have to come in from Anchorage, so we might get there before them, depending upon how far up into the mountains the incident is. We've been given the coordinates and Chuck is readying the vehicle now.'

'Pilot Chuck?'

'The very same. The guy knows this area like the back of his hand. He'll get us to where we need to go.'

'I guess I should be glad it hasn't been snowing and we're not going by dog sled.'

He smiled. 'It's a shame you'll be gone before any snow hits the ground. A dog-sled ride is something not to be missed.'

He was hauling equipment onto his back, so almost didn't notice the look of uncertainty on Charlie's face. The way it had changed when he'd said she'd be gone. It was almost wistful. Almost sad.

'Here. Take this.' He passed her a second go bag and then began to lead her to the back of the clinic where Chuck was apparently waiting.

'What do we know about the patient's injuries?'

'We don't know, but a fall into a crevasse could be anything. Broken bones, blood loss, loss of consciousness, hypothermia depending upon how long they've been out and exposed to the wild. Maybe dehydration?'

She nodded, hefting the bag higher onto her shoulder.

At the vehicle, he swung open the trunk and hauled in their equipment. 'You ever attend a field call?'

'Only during training. I did a shift with some paramedics.'

'In the wild?'

'No. Inner city.'

He smiled at her. 'Well, this is a little bit different, but don't worry. I'll keep you safe.'

'I'm glad to hear it.'

Chuck started the engine and began to drive them away from Vasquez and up into the mountain range. There was nothing to do but wait until they arrived, so Eli looked over at Charlie to see what she made of the scenery.

Her face was a mask of awe and wonder as the

urban signs began to drop away and they drove further into nature. The grey-purple mountains rose up all around them, thick with vegetation and, after one turn, the vehicle actually scared a group of three or four deer off the tarmac, sending them scattering into the trees.

'How you settling in, Doc?' Chuck asked her.

'Yeah, good, thanks. How are your dogs doing?'

'Good. Got a new litter of pups due soon.'

'Well, don't tell Alice.'

'Too late. I gave a talk at the school last week and she was there listening as I told her all about it. But don't worry, they're not the kind of dogs you'd want as a household pet. My dogs are working animals and they're made for the outside and pulling sleds and racing, not for lying on a couch and getting fat.'

Charlie nodded and glanced at Eli.

Every smile she gave him made him feel good inside. He wanted to reach out and take her hand in his, but Chuck was here and he didn't think she'd want anyone to know about how they felt about one another, or that they were in a relationship. It was crazy, really. They'd agreed to a fling with no strings, but hadn't actually done anything yet, but kiss. That goodbye kiss they'd shared after he'd spent the day with her and Alice... It had been tropical in its heat and seriously tempting him to break his promise to be a gentleman about this. And he wasn't actually sure how many other guys would agree to a fling with a woman and just be happy to spend time with her, without touching, and help her take care of her sick kid.

Because he'd been more than happy to do that. It had felt nice. As if they were a little family together. And he should have run a mile from that, because it was a dangerous road for him to travel down, hoping like that. Allowing his imagination to run away with all those fancy ideas of settling down with someone, maybe getting married, maybe having a family he could call his own. Because he'd never have that.

He couldn't give Charlie all those babies she'd said she wanted. He couldn't give her the big family she'd once dreamed of. If she got involved with him on a serious level? Then there would be no more pregnancies. No more babies. Alice would be her one and only child and he knew he couldn't do that to her.

So, he should have shut down those thoughts.

Should have turned tail and run. But being with Charlie was just so right and so good that she was a drug at this point.

So instead, he'd found himself lingering at her door, as they'd said goodnight.

He'd so wanted to stay. Had so wanted to suggest that he stay the night and he'd leave really early in the morning, but he'd refrained from doing so, because who knew if Alice would come into Charlie's room in the middle of the night with a tummy ache? What would have happened then? And maybe it was best for them if they just took each other in little bite sizes? So it didn't become overwhelming, so they didn't start getting ideas about each other that they shouldn't?

And so, before she'd opened the door to let him out, they'd stood there, together, staring into each other's eyes, their heartbeats feeling as though they were synced, and he'd gently cupped her face and kissed her softly. The longing he'd felt for her all day long contained in a single, gratifying, mind-blowing kiss.

'Goodnight, Eli,' she'd whispered, her voice husky and a little breathy afterwards.

'Goodnight, Charlie.' He'd swept his thumb over her bottom lip, stared at her mouth some more, imagining the wonders of those lips elsewhere, and then he'd torn himself away, every step that he took walking away from her house a torture.

He'd felt so comfortable there. So right. And maybe he was an incredible fool for letting his mind imagine the possibilities with her, but so be it. He couldn't help it. Charlie was different. Charlie was special and always would be.

It took them just under an hour before Chuck pulled over on a dirt road as a chopper circled overhead, looking for a space to land.

'Looks like we've both got here at the same

time. We'll head off on foot. Chuck, you've got the co-ordinates?'

'Sure have. It's this way,' he said, pointing towards a small dirt trail that led higher into the mountains, before he reached into his flatbed truck and opened up a metal case that contained a rifle. He pocketed some ammo and hauled the rifle over his shoulder. 'Let's go.'

'What's the rifle for?' Charlie asked, looking a little shocked.

'It's preventative.'

Chuck led the way, Charlie second, so that Eli could bring up the rear and keep an eye on her and keep her safe. There could be anything out here. Mountain lion. Elk. Wolf. Grizzly. All manner of creatures. That was the reason for the gun. If the patients had shed any blood, any kind of predator would have tracked that scent over many miles and be on their way too and no one would want to fight off a grizzly, or worse, without some kind of backup to scare off the predator before they could be rescued. The rifle was protection. Chuck wouldn't actually shoot an animal unless he absolutely had to. They weren't hunting here.

The steep incline was quite the workout for his calf muscles and he was glad of all the cardio he undertook. Charlie sounded out of breath and Chuck sounded as if he might be the one to need the oxygen, when suddenly the trail evened out and the pace got easier.

Chuck checked his map, looked out across the view and continued on down the path. It was getting quite rocky underfoot and the scrubby trees were becoming sparse as they began climbing over large boulders that seemed to block their way.

'Watch your footing, guys. You don't want to turn an ankle here,' Chuck advised.

They began to make their way along a ledge that had a stony path. Clearly this was a way up for some mountaineers. The path turned in and out of view, and after they'd been ascending for about ten minutes they saw a guy, dressed in red, waving his arms furiously and calling.

'Over here! We're over here! Jackie, Adam, they're here.'

Jackie and Adam must be the patients, Eli thought.

There was the temptation to rush these last few metres, but Chuck stopped them from pressing ahead too fast and made sure that Charlie kept the same pace they'd been walking at, until they reached the guy in red.

'Thank God you're here! Jackie slipped and fell down a crevasse. She was unconscious for a while, so we think she banged her head. Adam went down to rescue her, but was afraid to move her, so he's been trying to keep her awake and warm.'

'Any medical history we should know?'

'Jackie's just got the all-clear from breast cancer. She had a double mastectomy, chemo and radiation treatments over the last year.'

'Is she on any meds right now? Any allergies?'

'I don't think so.'

'Okay. Mountain Rescue are on their way. Is there a way that one of us can abseil down to Jackie?'

'Sure. We can attach one of you to our ropes.' The guy looked them over and kept his gaze on Charlie. 'It's gonna have to be you. The gap in the crevasse isn't big enough for anyone else.'

Charlie looked at him. 'I've never done anything like that before.'

She looked apprehensive.

'Don't worry. We'll talk you through it, every step of the way.'

She nodded and took note as Gerry, the guy in red, attached her to a harness, rope and karabiners. He gave her instructions on how to hold the rope, how to break, how to feed the rope through so that she would descend.

Eli attached a go bag to her harness with an extra karabiner. 'You're all set. You can do this,' he said, smiling at her, hoping that his encouragement would give her the belief that she needed. But he understood her reticence. She was a city girl. She'd never rock climbed or abseiled in her life and now she had to because someone's life depended upon it. He wanted to have the utmost confidence in her, but knew she'd be afraid.

So would he. He wanted to keep her safe and if it could be him to make his way down to the patient, he'd prefer it.

'Okay.'

She kept her gaze on him as she backed out towards the crevasse. Gerry wasn't joking, there was only a small narrow channel through the rock, which opened out into a bigger chamber below.

Eli looked over and down through the crevasse. It was a long drop. Charlie would have to rappel freely for quite a way and even though Adam was there beneath her at the icy, rocky bottom to help her break or slow down, if she lost control, he still felt apprehensive. Having to place his trust in a guy he didn't know.

He met Charlie's gaze. Saw the fear in her eyes. Nodded.

You can do this.

Her hands were trembling and he wanted to reach out and lay his hand on hers so much, to still them. To let her know he believed in her.

Something in his eyes must have given her the confidence, because suddenly she was moving away from him. Backwards and down, over the edge, hesitating slightly as she looked where to place her feet.

'That's it. Slow and steady.'

He watched her disappear from view and felt a lump of dread settle in his stomach. 'You okay?' he called out.

'I'm okay,' came back her voice, echoing around the rock.

He hated not being able to see her. To not view her progress, or lack thereof, and suddenly he wished they'd waited for Mountain Rescue. Surely they wouldn't have been much longer? They'd seen the helicopter hovering, knew they were close! But the fact that Jackie had lost consciousness and suffered a head injury had made them forge ahead to get a doctor down to her.

'How are you doing?' he called again, his stomach in absolute knots. He should never have let her go. She had a child! A daughter! She had someone who depended on her, he didn't. It should have been him. They could have found a way, surely?

There was no response.

'Charlie!'

A pause. Then, 'I'm okay! I'm nearly there! About ten more metres to go.'

Her voice echoed again and he'd never been so relieved to hear it. But then he heard something he didn't like.

A man's voice, calling out. 'Too fast! Watch out!'

There was the sound of a thud. Of a person hitting rock.

'Charlie!'

There was a cry of pain and he instantly felt sick. 'Charlie!' He spun around and faced Gerry. 'Hook me up. I don't care. I'll make it down there somehow.'

'You're too big.' Gerry looked sorry.

'Doc? I think the other doc has broken her leg or something!' called Adam.

Damn it!

He spun around, wanting to be with her. To scoop her up into his protective arms and take her someplace safe. But that was an impossibility. It wasn't just Charlie he had to worry about, but Jackie, too.

'How's Jackie?' he called.

'Conscious. Her head has stopped bleeding, but she can't remember much.'

'And she's breathing okay?'

'Yes, sir!'

'Okay, you need to get the oxygen out of the go bag and place the oxygen mask over Jackie's face,' he continued to yell.

'Already on it! Charlie here is already telling me what to do.'

He smiled with relief. That Charlie was still putting her patient first over herself was remarkable and proved just what kind of a doctor and person she was. Selfless. But then again, she always had been. Even as a kid, she'd helped out the other kids at the home. Especially the littler ones. Helping patch up their cuts and grazes and trying to cheer them up afterwards. She had to be afraid and in a great deal of pain herself, if it was true she'd broken something from her bad landing, but was still determined that Jackie would receive help first.

As he listened to what was going on at the bottom of the crevasse, he heard Chuck behind him. 'Rescue's here.'

He quickly got to his feet and summarised the situation to them.

Two of the rescue guys, small in stature, thankfully, hooked up some more ropes and began to abseil down the crevasse and Eli felt much better knowing that Charlie would also receive help.

The rescue guys had radios and had passed one to Eli before disappearing over the edge and when they got to the bottom, he was very much relieved to hear Charlie's voice. 'Hey.'

'Hey. How are you doing?' His voice softened.

'I'm all right. I got Adam to put a headcollar on Jackie and they're bringing her up now. I think she may have a broken arm or wrist, but it's the head injury that's the major concern.'

'And you? Run it down for me.'

He heard her sigh. 'Possible lower leg or ankle fractures.'

'Plural?'

'Yeah. Both hurt. My left leg has a noticeable

deformity about an inch above the ankle and the right one hurts like you wouldn't believe.'

'You did drop from a height onto rock. We'll get you X-rayed when we get you back to the clinic.'

'Take care of Jackie first.'

'I will take care of you both. Now, have you taken any of the painkillers?'

'No. I wanted to keep a clear head for Adam while I told him what to do.'

'Then do it now.'

'Yes, boss.'

He heard the slight smile in her voice and had to stop himself from cradling the radio. He couldn't hold *her*, but he could hold the item that was bringing him her voice. He hated the idea that she was hurt and lying at the bottom of the crevasse.

The mountain rescue guys ascended with Jackie, wearing a neck collar and with bandages wrapped around her head and one arm in a sling. The bandage on her head was bleeding through at the right temple and he attended to it by adding another pressure bandage to try and stop the bleeding. But they couldn't take any risks and now that Jackie was out of the crevasse, they were able to strap her to a back board. They would have to carry her back down the ravine towards where the truck was parked and then drive her to the helicopter, so she could be airlifted.

'Sending up Adam.'

Eli grabbed the radio. 'You first. You're injured.'

'I'm sending up Adam, Eli,' she replied more firmly, and before he could say anything else Adam's relieved face appeared as he was pulled back up.

'How is she?' he asked the man.

'Bloody amazing! She splinted her own legs, while telling me what to do!'

Eli stood over the crevasse and clicked the button on the radio. 'Tell me when you're ready.'

'I'm ready.'

Eli nodded to Gerry and they began to winch Charlie back up through the small gap in the crevasse. His heart was already pounding fast, but felt as if it went into tachycardia the second he spotted her rising up through the gap. She turned and her legs bumped against the rock on the edge and she winced, but Eli knelt and scooped her up into his arms and moved her away from the ledge.

'I'm fine. See to Jackie.'

'The rescue guys are already seeing to her. She's fine. Just concussed, I think. I couldn't feel any fractures. Let me look at you.'

'I'm fine and put me down!'

'I'm carrying you back to the truck.'

'That's a long way, Eli.'

'I'm a strong guy.'

As they spoke, the helicopter hovered above

them, brought in by the rescue team, who hooked up Jackie's scoop to a cable and she was airlifted up off the mountain. The downward pressure from the helicopter was intense, but thankfully they were sheltered by an overpass.

One of the rescue team turned to Eli. 'We don't have another scoop for her, but we can help you carry her down.'

'What about Jackie?'

'There's a driver and EMT waiting with the truck, so they'll be able to unhook Jackie and get her loaded into the helicopter.'

'Honestly, I'm fine,' Eli said.

'Mate, let us help you.'

Fair enough. There was no point in being proud and help would be appreciated, no matter how much he wanted to wrap his arms around her and protect her. But already his mind was racing. If one of her legs was broken, then that could be a problem, depending on the severity of the break. If both legs were broken? She'd be in a wheelchair for a while. Because even though he'd advise her to rest, he couldn't imagine her accepting that.

I can work from a wheelchair.

He could already imagine her saying it. But it wasn't just work, was it? What about Alice? What about getting her to school and home again?

The rescue guy and Eli joined hands to make a seat beneath Charlie's rear. She draped an arm around each of their shoulders and they began to make their way back down the ravine.

He couldn't stop himself from glancing at her. Checking her colour. Her respiratory rate. Whether she looked to be in pain. She had one break for sure and was putting a brave face on it. High pain threshold?

It took them some time to make it back to Chuck's truck, as they had to move slower, to make sure their steps were steady and they didn't trip over the numerous obstacles on the path—rocks, roots that emerged from the ground and dipped back in again like sea serpents, loose gravel, divots where rabbits, or some other burrowing animal, had decided to dig.

Chuck lowered the back end and they placed her onto the back of the truck.

Eli climbed on with her and settled beside her.

'What are you doing?'

'Riding with you.'

'I'm fine! You'll get bounced around back here. No need for us both to be uncomfortable.'

'This selfless nature of yours is endearing, but could you keep your trap shut for once? I'm riding in back with you, whether you like it or not.'

Her mouth opened as if to say something, but then clamped shut again.

Eli smiled. 'That's right. Jeez, doctors really are the worst patients.' He sat next to her and draped an arm around her shoulders. He felt her freeze initially and then she sank against him.

'Thanks.'

'You're welcome. I figured you might be cold and that's what I'll say if Chuck mentions it, okay?'

'What about when we drive into Vasquez?'

'I'll repeat it.'

Again she opened her mouth and shut it again, without speaking.

Chuck started the engine, backing up and turning around, giving the rescue boys a lift back to the helicopter. He dropped them off and they watched as the helicopter rose into the air, stirring up dust and dirt in whorls, before it inclined slightly and surged forward and away from the mountains.

'Jackie's going to Anchorage?'

'It's the best place for her, especially if she has a closed head injury. I couldn't feel one, but that doesn't mean there isn't one there.'

'She was a nice lady. Confused, but nice.'

'So, tell me, what happened during your descent?'

Charlie shrugged. 'I don't know. I was feeding the rope through like I was told and then Adam panicked because Jackie got sick and I tried to speed up, but the rope just whizzed through my grip, so then I got scared and couldn't remember which hand slowed me down and which one sped me up. Next thing I knew, I went crashing onto the rocks.'

'You didn't bang your head?'

'No. I landed on my feet.'

He leaned forward to examine the splints. 'You did these yourself?'

She nodded.

Eli looked right into her eyes. 'You're amazing, you know that, right?'

She flushed and this time he really saw it, because her skin had been pale to begin with. He liked that she was affected by his compliment.

'When we get to the clinic, we'll get you into X-Ray.'

'What if it's bad? What if I need surgery? I can't go back to Anchorage.'

'I've done my fair share of orthopaedics. In fact, I worked two whole years on an orthopaedic surgery ward and I worked with the best. If you need plates and screws, then I'm your man.'

'I could make a rude comment for that, but I won't.'

'Don't hold back on my account.' He grinned.

She smiled. 'I was going to say I bet you're good for more than just a casual screw.'

He raised an eyebrow and stared right at her, a smile touching his lips. 'You bet I am.'

'Your left tib and fib are fractured at the distal end, with a rotation. We should be able to twist them back into place and get you in a cast for a while. Your right ankle has a hairline fracture, which shouldn't need anything but rest.' Eli stood by her bed in the clinic, delivering the news.

'You're joking?'

'Nope.'

'Damn it.' How was she going to cope with everything if she had to be off her feet? 'I'll get about in a wheelchair for a bit. I can still work, just you watch.'

'And Alice? How will you get her to school? Cook for her? Clean up after her?'

'She's a capable girl. I raised her right. She'll help me.'

'She's five. She shouldn't have to be her mother's nurse and she'll be tired from having been at kindergarten all day. I have another solution.'

'I'm all ears.'

'I'll help you.'

Eli? Help her? 'How?'

'I'll move in for a bit. I can take Alice to school, drive us both to work, where you can be parked behind your desk all day, and then I'll take us home, cook dinner, help you bathe and get you into bed.' He grinned.

It felt as though her brain suddenly stopped working as her jaw practically hit the floor. Eli? Move in? 'No!'

'It's the perfect solution.'

'No, it's not. What would Alice think with you sleeping over?'

'She'll know that I'm there to help you both. I can sleep on the couch, if that's what you're worried about.'

'I'm not worried about you sleeping on the couch.'

'Good, because I could always sneak back to it, before Alice wakes.'

'No. She comes in my room sometimes. Clambers into bed with me in the middle of the night and I don't know about it, until I wake up.'

He shrugged. 'Then I'll just take my sweet time putting you to bed. Tuck you in nice and tight and stroke your brow until you fall fast asleep.'

'Eli—'

'I'm joking! I'm not going to take advantage of a woman who is incapable of standing on her own two feet.'

'Good.'

'Besides, I've heard bed baths are very entertaining these days.' He grinned.

'Eli!'

'Joke.' He looked around to make sure no one was watching, then leaned forward and kissed her on the forehead. 'It's just a joke. Unless…you *do* want me to give you a bed bath?'

'My hands work perfectly well and I will be more than capable of running a wet flannel over my body all by myself.'

His gaze travelled down her body. 'Shame.'

Honestly, he was exhausting! 'I'll let you stay and help out and I thank you for thinking of me and Alice, but in front of my daughter? In our home? My body is mine and you don't get to touch it, understood?'

He saluted her. 'Understood.'

'Good. Now go see if there's any update on Jackie.'

CHAPTER THIRTEEN

JACKIE, LUCKILY, DID not have a closed head injury, apart from concussion and the need for eight stitches to sew up her head laceration. She did, however, have a dislocated shoulder, a fractured wrist and a proximal break on her humerus—her upper arm bone.

The doctors in Anchorage had treated her with fluids and a couple of casts, but she would need surgery in the morning to help realign and plate her humerus. 'The shoulder has been reduced and the doctors have told me that they believe Jackie's lack of memory will improve after the concussion begins to dissipate.'

'That's great news,' Charlie said as he wheeled her into place at her dinner table.

They'd already collected Alice from kindergarten. His mom had been so surprised to see them turn up to collect Alice together, with Charlie in her wheelchair, and had been amazed at their story, smiling at them both and patting Charlie's hand. Alice, on the other hand, far from being scared about seeing her mom in a wheelchair, had thought it was cool and insisted on sitting on her mom's lap, all the way back to the truck.

'Can I have a go in it, Mom?'

'Maybe later.' She'd smiled, glad that her daughter hadn't been upset to hear of her mother's injuries. In fact, most perturbingly, Alice had been thrilled that Eli would be moving in for a while to help out. 'I can sell him another one of my drawings!'

As she sat at the table, she couldn't help but notice that Eli knew where everything was in her kitchen. He picked the right cupboard when he needed a saucepan. A right, yet *different* cupboard when he was looking for the strainer. 'How do you know where everything is?'

He looked over his shoulder at her with a smile as he reached up high for the cheese grater. 'This is my mom's, remember?'

'And?'

'Who do you think does all the maintenance?'

Of course. He'd fixed her drippy tap and everyone in Vasquez seemed to multitask with their jobs. It wasn't just them in their clinic. It was Chuck who drove ambulance trucks and bred and raced working malamute dogs. It was Eli's mom, who owned, not only this lodge, but the town's hotel and the town's diner and God only knew what else, while *also* being the kindergarten teacher!

'And what are you making for dinner?'

'Pasta.'

'Oh.' Well, that was easy. 'I thought you'd be an amazing chef, too, and not just pour something out of a packet.' It was good to know he wasn't an expert on human bodies *and* house repair *and* cooking.

'I'm making my own dough. You haven't tried real pasta until you've tried my goat's cheese and spinach ravioli.'

Huh.

He could cook, too. 'Where did you learn to cook?'

'My mom.'

'I like that you call her Mom.'

He shrugged. 'It's what she is. From the day they drove me home, I was made to feel like one of them. Like I'd always been there and that the missing years didn't matter.'

'Do they matter?'

He seemed to think for a minute. 'They do, but in a different way now. Those early years I was just trying to find my own way, not knowing where I wanted to steer to. Becoming a Clark gave me roots. It gave me guidance. And they've been there for me through every difficulty.'

Difficulty? 'Like medical school?'

He smiled. 'Yeah.'

She felt then in the way that he looked as if maybe he was referring to something else. The girl that walked away and left him? Who broke his heart? He'd mentioned her before, but didn't speak of her much. Lenore. What had happened there?

Charlie knew she could ask him, but would he answer? She didn't speak of Glen and what had happened with him. She just couldn't get the idea out of her head that once Eli knew the real truth, he'd go racing over to a computer and look up those pictures and she couldn't bear the idea of him seeing her like that. Vulnerable.

It was bad enough he was seeing her like *this*. In a wheelchair. It was hardly sexy, was it? This man had wanted a fling with her and she had wanted one with him, but it seemed that every time they tried to be together, something stopped them. Alice getting ill. Charlie abseiling badly. Broken ankles… And tonight he would be sleeping in her home. Just yards from her bedroom. How was that going to feel?

She gazed at the slope of his arm over his triceps. The way the muscles flexed as he kneaded dough. The way his hands forced the dough this way, then that. She could imagine his fingers tracing over her skin and she shivered.

'Cold? I can get you a blanket.'

He had a splash of white flour on his black tee, near his waist. She wanted to brush it away and feel those rock-hard abs beneath her fingers. 'No, not cold. I'm okay, thanks.'

'Shame.' He looked around them both, checked that Alice was absorbed somewhere in her bedroom, the door closed. 'I would have found a fun way to warm you up.' He winked at her and smiled naughtily.

Okay. She'd play along. Maybe this would have to be a fling with words only? 'How exactly?'

He raised an eyebrow at her, wiped his hands on a clean towel and then sauntered over towards her, leaning down low so that his hands rested either side of her on the wheelchair arms. 'First I'd make you close your eyes,' he whispered. 'Then I'd gently kiss you on the neck. Once. Twice. I'd breathe hot air over your goose-pimpling skin and then brush my lips over yours and then, baby? I'd make you forget the rest of the world.'

Her breathing had become heavy as she imagined each and every delicious image. A smile crept back onto her face. 'How?' She chuckled slightly, feeling incredibly naughty.

He grinned and placed one hand on the back of her neck, beneath her hair, and pulled her in close for a long, languorous kiss.

He wasn't lying. Kissing Eli did make her forget everything. The pain in her legs. Everything that had happened that day. All she could think was…*oh, my God!*

His hand slowly traced the line of her neck, one finger trailing down her chest bone and then circling around her breast to find her taut nipple that was thrusting against the material of her top. She ached—*physically ached*—to feel his skin against hers.

Damn this blouse! Damn this bra!

And then, when she felt as though she couldn't contain herself any more, he released her nipple and stopped kissing her and backed away, smiling.

And with perfect timing too!

Alice's bedroom door swung open. 'Mom, when is dinner ready?'

'Not long, Alice. Twenty minutes?' Eli said, looking perfectly innocent as he spoke to her daughter, while Charlie still sat in her chair, breathless and aroused.

'Okay.' Alice disappeared back into her bedroom.

Charlie met Eli's gaze. He looked happy. Smug. Normally she would want to wipe that smile off his confident face, but her brain wasn't really working well enough to come up with a retort. 'Erm...' She cleared her throat. Swallowed. 'Is there going to be a dessert?'

He grinned. 'There just may be.'

What is happening?

She watched him cut his pasta into squares and spoon little hills of goat's cheese and spinach onto them, before sealing them with another thin layer of pasta. Then he began chopping up some tomatoes, which he added to a sauce in a pan, grinding black pepper over the top.

Draping a dish towel over his shoulder, he then went to the fridge and pulled out some chilled moulds.

'What are those for?'

'Chocolate soufflés.'

Soufflés. That was risky. She'd watched enough cooking shows to know that the soufflé was feared. They either came out perfect or wrong. No in between. But she liked his confidence. That was something Eli had never been short of. Something she envied.

He poured some juice into a large jug that he added ice and slices of orange to and placed it on the table with three glasses. Then he placed the pasta into boiling water gently. 'Let's get you washed up,' he said.

'I can get myself to the bathroom sink. Alice! Time to wash your hands, please!'

She was glad of the cool water. It helped diffuse some of the heat she'd felt earlier when Eli had kissed her. When she reversed out of the bathroom, Eli was waiting for her.

'I can wheel myself.'

'You've just washed your hands. Let me push you.'

She let him guide her to the table, then he held out Alice's seat and draped a serviette over her lap, like a waiter in a posh restaurant. Alice giggled.

'Can I pour the young lady a drink?' he asked, bowing low.

Again, Alice laughed. 'Yes, please.'

After he'd done Alice's drink, he held the juice over Charlie's glass. 'Madam?'

'Please.' She smiled at him, feeling a real warmth towards him. He was putting in so much effort for her, but when hadn't he? Ever since she'd arrived here, he'd been there, helping out, always with a smile or a joke. He'd helped out when Alice was poorly. He'd been incredibly concerned when she'd got hurt and now he'd moved in to help them out.

What had she given him in return?

Feeling a little guilty, she watched him go and drain the pasta, before he transferred it into their bowls, with a helping of the tomato sauce. He brought the three plates over to the table, serving Alice first, then Charlie, then himself, before he sat down.

'Bon appetit.'

'Bon appetit.'

And, of course, it tasted absolutely delicious! The rich, succulent goat's cheese, the freshness of the spinach, the soft, thin pasta, all mixed with the spiced heat of the tomatoes that had a kick of chilli when it hit the back of your throat. But not so much that Alice couldn't eat it.

'Mom…there's a sports day happening soon, will you come?'

'Oh, sure, honey! Of course, I will. I wouldn't miss it.'

Alice smiled. 'Mrs Clark said that there's going to be a parents' race for mummies and daddies. Will you still be able to race in your wheelchair?'

'Oh, sorry, honey, but I don't think so. Maybe next time?'

'I could do it,' suggested Eli.

Charlie looked at him as Alice beamed. 'Yes! Please? Can Eli do it, Mom?'

'Well, I don't know…what would people think? He's not your daddy, sweetheart. It might be cheating,' she said, with a sympathetic smile and hoping Alice wouldn't push it, because what would people think? Eli running in a parent's place at the sports day? The rest of Vasquez would be there. Would it start any gossip? Or had that horse already bolted? People would soon know that he'd moved in to help out. They might assume something anyway.

'I don't think it's cheating, Mom.'

'Nor me,' said Eli, grinning at Alice and dabbing at his mouth with his napkin.

His helpful addition did not go unnoticed. She gave him a look. 'It's a *parents'* race and you're *not* her parent. Thank you for the offer, but I don't think we should do it. You should save your strength and speed for when you have children of your own.'

A look crossed his face that she couldn't read, because it came and went so fast and then he was taking his plate back into the kitchen.

She felt somehow that she'd upset him, but didn't understand why.

He was clattering about. Whisking the chocolate, filling the ramekins, and then wiping the rims with a clean finger, before he placed them into the oven and set a timer for ten minutes.

Charlie put her and Alice's plates onto her lap and wheeled herself into the kitchen and placed them down next to the sink, so she could position herself to open up the dishwasher. But she couldn't quite get the angle.

'Let me.'

'No, it's fine, I can do it.'

He sighed and stepped back and she could feel his eyes on her as she lowered the door, put in the plates and then lifted the door back, shoving it closed.

'Are you okay?' she asked.

'I'm fine!' he said with a smile, before checking his watch.

'You don't need to check your watch. You've set a timer.'

'I know I have.'

'I've upset you, haven't I?'

He shook his head with a smile forced onto his face. 'Nope!'

'I have. When I said you should wait to become a parent yourself. I wasn't trying to imply that you were trying to steal my child or adopt her or anything.' She checked to make sure Alice couldn't hear. 'Or imply that our relationship is anything but what it is.'

'I know that.'

'Then why are you upset?'

'I'm not.'

'I don't believe you.'

'Look, it was just a race. I thought I could be Alice's champion. She's a great kid and she's excited about sports day. Or I could be your champion. Whichever way you want to look at it, that's all I wanted to be. To step in and save the day. To let Alice have someone she could cheer for at the race. I didn't want her to feel left out. It should just be a bit of fun, that's all. I don't happen to think that anyone will read anything into it. And if they did? So what?'

'Well, that's easy for you to say,' she said quietly. 'You've not been the centre of gossip before.'

He raised an eyebrow. 'You don't know that.'

She groaned. 'Okay, so everyone probably talked about the Clarks when they adopted you. Big deal. That's positive talk, nothing horrible. And maybe they talked when you and Lenore broke up. Big deal. You don't know what nasty gossip feels like.'

'Actually, I do. But it sounds, right now, like we're not actually talking about me, but talking about you.' He glanced over at Alice, who was absorbed with the television blaring away behind her. 'You've been the subject of malicious gossip?'

She coloured, thinking of Glen and what he'd done. It hadn't been Charlie's fault. She'd thought she was in a loving relationship to begin with, but it had all turned sour.

'It was a while ago and I don't need people talking about me again.'

Eli glanced at his soufflés.

They were rising nicely, of course.

'If you want, we can talk about this later?'

She nodded. Maybe it was time? She didn't have to tell him *all* the details. It might be nice to tell someone how she felt about it all. So far, she'd kept it all hidden deep inside, where it had begun to fester. But she had been thinking about how it might feel to share her problem with him. Share the burden.

He gave her a wink.

Hesitantly she smiled back.

When the soufflés were done, Eli served the biggest to Alice. 'Be careful. That small little dish is hot.'

They were a delight! Rich and chocolatey,

without being too sweet. The perfect accompaniment to his ravioli pasta parcels. Good-looking, sexy, intelligent, kind, considerate, a good cook, an excellent baker, an amazing kisser. Was there anything he was bad at? Or even moderately bad at? There had to be something. A man wasn't wrapped up in such an amazing parcel, like Eli, without there being something! She just figured she hadn't discovered it yet. The only clue she had was that he'd had a relationship sour and his girlfriend had left. Why? Was it because of something he'd done? Or *hadn't* done? Maybe it was because he was always joking around and laughing? Maybe she'd thought he couldn't take anything seriously?

Leaving Alice to watch the television after dinner, Eli wheeled Charlie out into the garden and sat down on a seat next to her. 'So…spill the beans. What happened to you?'

CHAPTER FOURTEEN

'IT'S ALL TO do with Alice's father.'

'Glen? Okay.' He wasn't sure what the man might have done to result in Charlie being the subject of bad gossip.

'He was perfect when we met. A bit like you, actually. Handsome, charming, suave. Great to look at. What people call a real catch. We just hit it off and we married early and I was head over heels in love. Or I thought it was love. Looking back now, I think it was just infatuation that this great guy wanted to be with me.'

'You're a great catch too. He was lucky to be with you.' He meant it.

'Thanks. Things were great to begin with, but I noticed little things that, on their own, weren't too concerning, but added together threw up a few red flags.'

'Such as?'

Charlie turned to make sure the patio door was closed, so that Alice couldn't hear. 'He was a se-curity guy. Dealt with tech and private home security. He worked for a company that installed cameras and alarms in people's property. Mansions, even. They were top notch. Glen always seemed a little on edge about people knowing our business. I felt it was just because of his job, you know? I thought he was just trying to protect me and at first, I thought it was great, you know, that he cared so much.'

'I'm sensing a *but*…'

'But it was low-level control of me. *"Are you really going to wear that dress at work?" "You look better without make-up." "I don't think you should hang around with Suzie any more, she said horrible things about me."'*

'He was isolating you.' Eli could feel ire building. He'd met a couple of controlling men in his time. There were one or two in Vasquez.

'Yes. But I've always been isolated. I have no family. I have no friends. I've never settled anywhere, until I met him, and he made me feel like he could give me everything I ever wanted in life—stability. A future. Start a family. The works. You know how much I've always wanted a big family of my own.'

He nodded, feeling a pang. Because he wanted the same thing too and couldn't have it.

'He wanted us to try for a kid straight after we married and one morning I woke up feeling sick and took a test. I was pregnant with Alice and that's when Glen changed big time.'

'How so?'

'He just seemed… I don't know…upset at the attention I got from people because of my growing bump. He tried to say it was because he didn't want people fawning over me, touching my belly, because how was I to know whether they had a knife or not? Whether they were dangerous or not? He began telling me to stay at home and I pretty much only left the house to go to work, OBGYN appointments and scans.'

'And…people at your work were noticing?'

'They told me I was beginning to look ill. Pale. Withdrawn. And I guess it was because I didn't want to attract attention, because I knew it would just send Glen into a funk. He didn't hit me or call me names or anything. He kept saying it was just concern for my well-being. But his silences were legendary and I couldn't bear the silence and I would find myself doing anything I could to make him happy again.'

'And you didn't like the talk, because people at work were concerned for you?' It didn't seem that this would be enough to have upset her as she'd seemed.

'No, that wasn't the problem. Glen became even more controlling. Wanted me to give up work, stay at home. He monitored my phone, checked all my messages, questioned me over everything. And then one night, I noticed I was spotting. I was about six months pregnant and very scared, but Glen wouldn't let me go to get checked out. He said he didn't want a man looking at me like that, or examining me. I said I'd ask for a woman, but he still wasn't happy. He locked the doors.'

'You're kidding me?'

She shook her head. 'I'd put up with his behaviours for far too long and when we left to see his mother the next day, I escaped through a bathroom window and went straight to a hospital.'

'Was everything okay?'

'Just a breakthrough bleed. But I couldn't believe he'd possibly endangered the life of our child and put me through a sleepless night, just because he was so paranoid. So I left him. I had nowhere to go. Nowhere to live. I got a cheap room at a motel and that's when everything went incredibly bad.'

'It wasn't *already* bad?'

'He shared things that he shouldn't,' she said, not feeling brave enough to say it straight out.

Eli frowned. 'I don't understand.'

'He…um…he'd had secret cameras around the house.' She glanced at him, judging how much to say. Wanting to say it straight out, afraid of his reaction. 'Ones I didn't know about…in the bedroom…and he'd made videos and taken photos of me when I was naked and…' she paused a long time '…posted them online.'

She couldn't look at him then, afraid to see the

shock on his face. Afraid to see the pity. Or what if she saw something worse? Curiosity? Wonderment. A need to see these pictures for himself? They were in a relationship after all. A strange one, maybe, but perhaps he'd feel possessive, too? And she couldn't bear to see that on his face.

But then she heard him shift in his seat and suddenly he was kneeling before her, her hand in his, and he had to reach up to gently guide her face to turn to his. 'That should never have happened to you. This Glen…he should be the one to feel ashamed. Not you. Did you call the police?'

She nodded, tears forming in her eyes, burning them. 'They got him to take the stuff down, but people can make copies. Save it. They are still out there and I have to live with that and raise a daughter to believe that nothing can bring her down, and yet she lives in a world where men can do this to women and justify their actions to themselves. How do I tell her that? How do I teach her to protect herself, when we live in a world where there are cameras watching us always?'

'You teach her to always be on the alert, but that there are good men out there, too. Men who will respect her if she chooses not to consent. If she chooses to say no. You teach her to live a life well-lived and not one that resides in fear.'

'You mean like me? I live in fear, because of what Glen did. I ran away, unable to cope with the influx of harassment I got after those things went public. I moved. I kept on moving, even when I had Alice, afraid to settle anywhere, afraid to let people know me, in case they found out. And now I've told you, I'm afraid that you will look at me differently.'

He smiled at her. 'I will always look at you the same way. That before me is the most beautiful woman I have ever seen in my entire life. A clever, kind, compassionate woman. An excellent mother. A brilliant doctor. An...' he grinned '...incompetent abseiler. But!' He chuckled and stroked her face. 'Never a victim. Because you fight for everything. You may have moved around, but you stand your ground when you are right. You love your daughter and try the best for her every day. You keep her safe and, in my opinion, she has the best role model a young girl could ever have.'

Charlie made a strange noise. Somewhere between a laugh, cry and a hiccup. But then she leaned forward in her chair and kissed him on the cheek. Quickly. Briefly. Glancing back through the patio doors to make sure that Alice hadn't seen. 'You're a good man, Eli.'

He winked at her, smiling. 'I try.'

Her legs ached, from the injuries, but also from the fact that, normally, she was an active person and this forced sitting down that she was having to do was becoming frustrating. As she sat listening to a patient, she made a mental note to herself that when she saw Eli, she'd ask if she could use crutches, somehow, instead.

He'd been amazing last night, listening to what she had to say, and she had to admit to herself that even though telling him had first felt as if it were the last thing she'd ever do, now that she had? It felt amazing. As if a weight had lifted and she knew now, in her heart, that Eli would not go looking for those images of her if they still existed somewhere in some dark recesses of the web. In fact, she actually believed that even if he did come across them, he would report them and track down the owners and forcibly have them removed on her behalf.

He'd been appalled at Glen.

But he had not judged her for trusting him. Because that was what you did in relationships, wasn't it? You trusted the other person. You gave them the benefit of the doubt. And if that relationship was an important one? As hers had been? Then you forgave people for little discrepancies in their behaviour in case they were having a bad day, or were acting a little out of character, because they just might be stressed. Glen's overprotective nature had seemed cute, at first. She'd loved that he wanted to keep her safe.

She just hadn't realised to what extent he'd been monitoring her.

'…and Chuck was out feeding the dogs and so he didn't see anything. It was all over by the time he came back in.'

Her patient was Chuck's wife, Angela. She'd come in that morning, after experiencing something odd at home.

'I don't normally come to the docs. You can see from my chart, I think the last time I was here was, ooh, a good five years ago and I've always been fit and well.'

'And did you experience anything else with the dizzy spell?'

'The room spun. I felt it *and* saw it. It made me feel incredibly sick and I began to panic a bit, to be honest with you.'

'And when this happened…had you bent down, or were you in a strange position? Or just standing normally when it happened?'

'Just standing. I was doing the breakfast dishes at the sink.'

'Looking down?'

'Yes. I was scrubbing the frying pan. We'd just had eggs.'

'And did you fall, or sway? What happened?'

'I squeezed my eyes shut, so I couldn't see it spinning. I could still feel it though, for just a few seconds and then it felt like it might have stopped, so I opened my eyes and the room was still again, but my heart rate was fast, I felt incredibly sick and shaky and so I made my way over to the kitchen chair and sat down.'

'And then Chuck came back in?'

'Yes. He said I was white as a sheet.'

'And did you have a headache at all?'

'Afterwards, yes. For about a half-hour.'

'Do you normally get headaches?'

'Not really. Not unless I haven't slept much.'

'Okay. Well, it could be an inner ear infection, so I'll check your ears first, okay?'

'Okay.'

'Any history of ear problems?'

'No. I've always been as fit as a fiddle.'

Charlie got out the otoscope and looked in Angela's ears, but both were clear. No wax build-up and no sign of infection. The eardrums looked exactly as they should. 'Any colds, recently? Sore throat?'

'No.'

'Ever get Covid?'

'Didn't everybody?'

'And how were you with that?'

'Fine! Just a cough for about a week. A bit of tiredness, but nothing bad.'

'I'd like to do an Epley manoeuvre, if that's okay? Just to see if it's debris in the ear canals moving around causing you to feel dizzy.'

'Okay.'

'But I'll need to call in Eli. I can't do it myself in this chair.'

'Fine. It'll be lovely to see him, I haven't seen him in a while…probably not since he got sick when he was still a student.'

Charlie frowned. Eli was sick? It couldn't be anything serious, surely? He seemed fine right now. She dismissed it and typed an instant screen message that would send to Eli's computer. Seconds later, she got a reply. He'd be right in.

'He's coming.'

'Bless him. He's a good man.'

'He is. The best.'

Angela looked at her, head tilted to one side in question. 'You're enjoying working together?'

'I am.'

'Vasquez is such a strange place. It must have taken some getting used to?'

'It's been great, actually. Eli and the Clarks and everyone here have been most welcoming.'

'And you get on well with Eli?'

'I think everyone does,' she said, laughing.

Angela smiled. 'He makes it easy. Mind you, it certainly helps that he's so easy on the eye, wouldn't you say?'

Charlie blushed.

'I thought so!' Angela preened with her point having been made, just as Eli rapped his knuckles on her door and came in.

'Angela! How are you?' He smiled at her patient.

'Fine. Just this dizzy spell that was worrying.

I think Chuck thought I might have had a TIA, or something, so best to get it checked out.' A TIA was a transient ischaemic attack. Sometimes called a mini stroke, in which effects of a stroke occurred for a short period of time and then dissipated, leaving no sign it had ever happened. Visually, anyway.

'Ears are normal, BP is spot on. I thought we could do an Epley?' Charlie said.

Eli nodded. 'No problem. Angela, would you be a darling and hop up onto the examination bed for me?'

'Of course.'

Once Angela was on the bed, Eli held her head in his hands and then turned it forty-five degrees to her left and then quickly lowered her to a prone position in which her head was lower than her body over the edge of the bed. Then he turned her head ninety degrees to the other side, watching her eyes all the time for signs of nystagmus—an involuntary movement of the eyes—then asked Angela to rotate her body so it was in alignment with her head, before sitting her up again, with her head still turned to the side. 'Feel anything?' he asked.

'No.'

'Let's do the other side.'

He repeated the procedure, but nothing happened. No nystagmus was reproduced.

'I want you to replicate the stance you were in when it happened,' Charlie suggested.

Angela did so, but again, nothing occurred.

'It might be worth doing some bloods, just a general MOT, see if that flags anything and if not, then we can put it down to being idiopathic in nature. But if you get dizzy again, Angela, I want you to call me right away, okay?'

'Okay. What will you check for in the bloods?'

'A full blood count, blood sugars, thyroid, electrolytes are considered standard in these cases.'

'All right.'

Charlie gathered together the things she would need and procured a quick sample from Angela's arm. 'You go home and take it easy for the day.'

'Are you kidding me? With all those dogs, a house and a husband to look after? Not to mention I've got the grandkids coming over. We've promised them a movie night.'

'Well, maybe let Chuck organise the grandkids?' Charlie smiled.

Angela laughed. 'We'll see.'

'Just take it easy, okay?'

Angela nodded and left the room.

Charlie turned to Eli. 'Thank you for helping out. I hope you weren't busy?'

'Not at all. How are you doing?'

'It's frustrating being in the chair. I'm not used to letting people do things for me that usually I'm capable of doing for myself.'

He nodded. 'I get that. I had it too, once.'

'You ever break your ankles?'

'Not quite. I got sick once and they brought me home from medical school. The Clarks looked after me. Fetched my shopping. Cooked my food. Mom practically never left my side for weeks.'

That had to be what Angela had mentioned. 'What were you sick with?'

'I don't really like to talk about it. It's gone now. No need to worry.' He smiled. 'Well, I'd better be off.'

And then he left her room so abruptly, she was left shocked into silence. No secret cuddle? No secret kiss? Something was most definitely off and she didn't like not knowing. The least he could do was open up to her, the way she'd opened up to him. She felt closer to him now. They were in a relationship in which they could confide their secrets. Their fears. Why wouldn't he share?

Wheeling her chair forward, she began to go after him. There were no more patients scheduled and she was due a break anyway. She found him in his office, staring out of the window. 'What's wrong, Eli?'

He turned. Smiled. 'Nothing!'

'No, you're lying to me. Something *is* wrong and I want you to feel that you can talk to me about anything. The way I talked to you. I told you something about me last night that I swore to never tell you, but I did so because I thought that...' she sighed, unsure as to whether to admit this '... I thought that maybe we weren't actually having a fling and that instead we were in some kind of relationship. One that involved feelings, because I don't know how to explain what else we have here. I mean, we haven't even, you know, slept together yet and yet I feel closer to you than I have to anyone in a long, long time.'

He looked down at the ground, then back up at her when she began speaking again.

'Flings don't help their bit on the side care for their sick child. They don't stay with them all day just to keep them company and then say that they've had a really nice time. They don't come round and cook. They don't move in when that fling has a stupid accident at work. They don't buy their daughter's artwork and buy them teddy bears. They don't look at me the way that you look at me.'

'I know. But we share a past, you and I. We're not just strangers.'

'No, we're not. But what are we, Eli? Is this simply a thing that goes one way? Am I the fool for thinking that you might feel more for me? Am I the idiot for confiding in you my deepest, darkest, shameful secret, when you won't tell me yours? Am I *deluded*?'

'Of course not.'

'Then why won't you speak to me and tell me

what's wrong? How can I feel any of the things I feel for you, if you won't let me know you?'

'You do know me.'

She shook her head. 'No, I don't. After you left? This life you've built? I hardly know anything about it. You got taken in by the Clarks, you had a seemingly mysterious illness you won't talk about and you had a relationship fail, but I don't know the ins and outs of your life. You don't share *anything*. You keep me on the edge and that's not how I want to be! If I'm going to be in someone's life, then I want to be in it. Heart and soul. I deserve that and I can't be with a man who wants to keep his secrets. Because I've been there, Eli. You know I have and look how that turned out for me.'

'I don't have cameras, Charlie. I'm not Glen.'

'But you have something you won't talk to me about,' she challenged him. Staring him down. Waiting for him to lower his gaze, but he didn't. He simply stared back at her and she realised that he was admitting that she was correct. Yes. There was something. 'I see. Then this?' She gestured between them. 'Is over. I can't stay here and look at you every day and pretend that we're close, when clearly we are not. I was a fool to stay here when I found out it was you. I should have trusted my instincts.'

'What are you saying?'

'I'm saying I'll find something else. Another

job. Someplace else. The second my contract here is over, I'm gone!'

'But Alice is settled here! Are you really going to keep hauling her around the country every few months because of a few pictures? What kind of life is that?'

'It's better than what we had.'

'Is that what you want for her? Something that's a little bit better than awful? Or do you want her to have a happy life? A future? In a place where she could build it?'

'What do you mean?'

'She has skills. Way beyond those of a normal five-year-old. She can draw. And here in Vasquez there is so much she could capture.'

'So you want me to stay so my daughter can draw some grizzlies, is that it? Way to go, Eli. Way to go in giving me an astounding reason to stay!' Now she felt angry. How could she ever have believed that this man would ever be serious with her? He never had been and all she'd been was fun to him. A plaything. Someone to entertain him for a bit. 'And how dare you imply that our lives were awful before? You know nothing about us!'

He stared at her then and nodded. 'You're right. I know nothing about you. Nothing that matters.' He turned and walked away and she was so shocked by it, she just sat there, staring at the empty space where he had once been.

CHAPTER FIFTEEN

THE DRIVE TO pick up Alice from kindergarten was tense. Charlie had insisted on getting into the truck all by herself and it had been quite the sight to see, seeing as the truck was higher than the wheelchair. But she'd come armed, he'd seen. Bringing with her some crutches to help support her body weight as she transferred from the chair to the truck. He'd itched to help her, but had known that if he'd tried, he would only have been sworn at or shook off and so, instead, he'd stood back, patiently waiting while it took her over two minutes to finally haul herself into the front passenger seat of his truck. She'd held the crutches tightly, so he'd taken the wheelchair, folded it up and placed it in the back of the truck.

Driving over to the school, he could have cut the tension in the vehicle with a chainsaw. But what could he do? Talk about it? What was there to say? Was there even a point to saying anything? What they'd had never even got properly started, it sure as hell was never going to last.

Charlie would leave with Alice. In every iteration of this scenario she would leave and be gone
for ever. Maybe he'd get the occasional email? A
Christmas card at best. So it was probably best
to just let this burn on out. They'd manage somehow, tensions would finally ease. Probably just as
she was about to pack up and go anyway.

He was used to people leaving him. He'd hard-
ened his heart to it. It was the only way to survive. He'd left her behind once, now it was only
right and fair that she had a turn.

He left Charlie in the truck when he went to
collect Alice. Normally they would meet her together in the schoolyard and listen to Alice nat-
ter about her day on the way back to the truck,
examining paintings or models she'd made, or
hearing her chat about something they'd done,
or which friends she'd made.

Alice came running out of her class, as usual,
with a broad smile upon her face. 'Eli!' She
slammed into him and he whisked her up in the
air with a broad smile and, laughing, twirled her
around, before putting her down again. God, he
would miss this kid!

'Good day?'

'The best! Mrs Clark was telling us about a
school trip that's coming up!'

'Oh, yeah? Where to?' He knew where to. His
mom took the kids up to the reindeer farm on Elk
Ridge each year. They had a small visitor and

education centre there, next to a much larger animal rescue and convalescence place.

'We're going to see some reindeer! And elk and bears and owls and all kinds of animals, Mrs Clark says!'

He smiled, knowing how much Alice would love the place. 'It's gonna be wild, huh?'

'It's in September. Think Mom will let me go?'

September. Ah. Charlie's contract ended in August. 'I don't know. You'll have to ask her.'

'Is she here? Why didn't she come with you?'

'Her legs were bad. She, er…wanted to wait in the truck to rest for a little while. It's been a long day at work, so…' He *hated* lying to her. He'd never lied to a kid, if he could help it, because he remembered how much it had hurt when adults had lied to him as a child. Mostly with making promises they knew they could never keep. Okay, so the lies weren't big, right now, but it could be a slippery slope.

'Oh. Okay. She must be in a lot of pain, then, because she always comes.'

He thought of the pained look he'd seen in Charlie's eyes when they'd been arguing. The hurt he'd seen, because she felt that their relationship was all one-sided.

She was wrong. But how could he tell her that?

Best to let her think that it was true. Then she could walk away at the end of all of this without guilt. If she walked away hating him, then that was better than walking away knowing he couldn't give her what she'd always wanted.

He held Alice's hand as she skipped back to the car to keep up with his longer strides. He liked this part. This part was nice. Where he could pretend he was her father.

This must be what it feels like.

He felt a huge pang then of longing. So close to what he wanted, but so far away.

He wanted to harden his heart. Letting go of her hand and not allowing himself to have such thoughts would be better for him when they walked out of his life for good. Pretending to be Alice's dad? Only pain waited for him in that iteration of life.

As they got to the truck, he opened up the back passenger door and lifted Alice in.

'Hey, Mom! Are you okay? Do your legs hurt?'

'I'm okay, baby, don't you worry,' Charlie answered.

He buckled her in and closed her door, then he got back behind the driver's wheel. 'Home?'

'Yay!' Alice said as he started the engine. 'Mom…there's a trip to see reindeer and all these other animals in September with Mrs Clark and my class. Can I go? Please?'

'Sounds great, baby, but I don't think we'll still be living in Vasquez when it gets to September. You'll be in a new school.'

'But I *love* my school. I love Mrs Clark. I love living *here*. Can't we stay here?'

Charlie turned around in her seat. 'There won't be a job for me, baby. The one I have now is only temporary, remember?'

Glancing through the rear-view mirror, he could see a sulk settle onto Alice's face. 'Not fair!'

'I'm sorry, honey.'

He wanted to make it better. He wanted to fix it. He didn't like seeing Alice upset and he hated not being able to talk to Charlie about it. But she was right. There wasn't a job for her. Not unless Nance chose to stay at home and not return to her old post. She might, even though she'd always said she would come back. But Ryan was Nance's first baby and who knew how she might feel about returning to work, now that Ryan was born?

Unable to do or say anything that would help, he drove them home in silence, fetching Charlie's wheelchair when they parked outside her place and standing awkwardly, yet again, as she stubbornly alighted from his truck, down to the seat in silence.

Inside, he went straight to the kitchen, while Charlie helped Alice get changed. He knew he needed to keep busy, or he'd go insane, so he gathered all the ingredients to make a chicken pot pie and began making shortcrust pastry.

He knew the secret to a good shortcrust was to make sure the butter was cold as he proceeded to rub it into the sifted flour with his fingers, to make it a breadcrumb texture. Then he added milk, slowly, until it formed a dough. He wrapped it in cling film and placed it in the fridge, pulling out the chicken breasts so he could chop them into bite-size chunks. It helped to keep busy. It helped to form the dough. It allowed him to not think too hard about what he was having to let go of.

'You don't have to cook.'

He turned to face Charlie. 'No offence, but I don't think you'd be able to do this on your own.'

'Well, that's just it, Eli. I can do everything on my own. It's all I've ever done. Occasionally I've let someone into my life and each time it has been an unmitigated disaster. To be honest with you, I'd feel much more comfortable in my home if I didn't have to see you all the time. I'll finish whatever this is and you can go and pack your things.'

He stared at her. 'You want me to go?'

CHAPTER SIXTEEN

'*You want me to go?*'

Yes, she did. Because it hurt to have him around. It hurt that he wouldn't open up and share his innermost feelings with her. Because he thought if he kept his distance, he wouldn't get hurt.

Turns out that maybe neither of us has changed our ways since we were small.

She'd been vulnerable and though, in the moment, it had felt good to share, now it felt truly awful. There was an imbalance in their relationship and she didn't like how it left her feeling weak and exposed. Because she'd been exposed before and wouldn't be so ever again.

'I can make a pie, or whatever this is.'

'It's a pie.' He continued to stare at her, as if weighing her up. As if deciding to say something else. But then she saw the decision in his eyes that he wasn't going to and he turned away and washed his hands to rid them of the flour. 'I'll pack up now.'

'I'll find a way to get Alice to school tomorrow, you don't have to do it.'

'But—'

'And I'll find a way to work, too.'

He sighed and dried his hands on a towel. 'Fine.' He grabbed his holdall from by the front door and began moving around the place, picking up his stuff. His hoodie from the back of the chair. His toothbrush and toiletries from the bathroom. All thrown into the bag. A book he'd been reading that was on the coffee table.

She'd got used to those things. He hadn't been living with her long, but it had become surprisingly nice how much she liked seeing his things about the place. Seeing them gone felt weird. As if the place was emptying somehow, which was ridiculous.

'I'll see you at work, then.' He stood by the door.

'Yes, you will.'

'Can I say goodbye to Alice?'

Honestly? She just wanted him to be gone. So she could get to the end of this unpleasantness. But she knew how much Alice would complain if he left without saying goodbye. 'Sure.'

'Alice?' he called.

Alice came out of her room, smiling. A smile that faltered when she saw him holding his bag and standing by the door. Perhaps she could even sense the tension in the room. 'Are you leaving?'

'Yeah. Come here and give me a hug.'

'But I don't want you to leave! Mom! Tell him to stay!' she pleaded, tears welling up in her eyes.

Charlie felt awful. This was why she never let guys get close. This was why guys never met her daughter. Because of this moment right here. 'He has to go, honey.'

'But, why?' she cried, slamming her little body into Eli's as he hefted her up into his arms and squeezed her tight.

Alice wrapped her little legs around his waist and cried into his shoulder.

'You'll see him again, some time. It's not like he's leaving Vasquez.'

But Charlie wasn't sure she was heard. Alice was crying so loudly. So hard.

The look on Eli's face was pained, his eyes closed as he held her little girl. It looked painful for him too, and she hated to see that. It made the guilt worse. She'd not expected this. For him to get close to her daughter. But he had.

'Come on, baby. Let him go.'

'No!' Alice cried, squeezing ever tighter.

'Alice? Alice, I want you to listen to me. Look at me. Alice?' Eli pulled back, until Alice looked up at him with a red, tear-streaked face. 'I'm just going back to my place. That's all. You'll still see me around.'

Alice shook her head, as if she didn't believe him.

'I promise you, you will see me around. Okay? Because I need to see all those fabulous drawings you do. I want to be able to say to people, *Oh, you like Alice Griffin's art? I knew her since she was a little kid. I bought the very first piece she ever sold!*'

Alice sniffed and managed a short smile.

'Let go, Alice,' Charlie said as Eli lowered her daughter to the ground.

'Can I walk with you to your truck?' Alice asked.

Eli glanced at Charlie and she looked away. Unable to meet his gaze. She felt awful. That Alice was getting hurt because of this? Of her mistake? Of letting Eli get close?

'Sure.'

She watched from the doorway, witnessing another painful hug, whispered promises and then watching her daughter cry as Eli got in his truck and drove away.

Charlie hoped that now that he'd gone, it would be easier.

She was wrong.

Alice stomped up the path and yelled at Charlie as she passed. 'You always spoil things!' And then she slammed her bedroom door, with the ferocity of a teenager.

Charlie sat there, blinking, unsure of how she'd

even got herself into this mess in the first place. But it was clear. Coming here to Vasquez, staying, once she knew Eli was here, had been a tremendous mistake.

Charlie had not arrived at work at her usual time, and he knew because for the last hour he'd stared alternately at the clock and then out of the window of the clinic, trying to work out what he would say to her when she got there.

An apology. That would be first. Clear. Profound. Touching. He'd let her know that he deeply regretted upsetting her. That he was upset that he had hurt her. And that he would understand if she wanted to be angry with him, but that he hoped that they could put it behind them while they worked together.

His cell rang in his back pocket.

Charlie? Ringing to apologise for being late? She was trying to do everything herself from that wheelchair.

But no. It was his mom.

Odd. Isn't she in class?

'Mom? Everything okay?'

'Well, no. I'm confused, honey. Charlie has pulled Alice from the school—she notified the office first thing and I've only just been told. Has something happened?'

She'd pulled Alice out of kindergarten? 'Oh… er…we had a bit of a falling out.'

'What kind of falling out?'

'We were…um…kind of…seeing one another. But…secretly…like a bit of fun.'

'Did she know it was just a bit of fun?'

And that was when he realised that it hadn't been *a bit of fun* for either of them.

Eli groaned. 'I did something stupid.'

There was a pause while his mom digested this. 'Is it something you can fix?'

'She wants kids, Mom. I can't give her that. Why keep her here when I can't give her the one thing she wants?'

'Honey…well, she wouldn't have been in a relationship with you, if she wanted that. Unless, of course, you didn't exactly tell her? I know you, Eli, better than you realise and you need to understand that sometimes you act like you haven't quite grown up properly.'

She always did have a polite way of telling him off. Mild chiding. Like a proper mom. He smiled briefly, glad to have found his mom in life, if he couldn't have anyone else. 'I couldn't tell her.'

'Why? Hasn't she always been special to you?'

'How do you know that?'

'Oh, honey, I heard the way you talked about her, even before she came here. I saw it in your eyes. She's something special and you'd be a fool to let her get away, without telling her everything.'

'I don't know if I'm brave enough.'

'You're the bravest guy I know. All you've been through? But tell me this…how scared are you of the idea of a future without her in it?'

He let out a breath. 'Terrified. There will always be something missing.'

She sighed. 'The piece of your heart you left behind with her, when you left the first time. When we took you from her.'

'You think she'd want me?'

'I think you should give her the option. Tell her the truth and let her decide, because if you don't, then you'll always regret it. If you tell her and she still wants to go, then at least you will know that you tried and she said no, knowing *all* the facts.'

His phone beeped. Another incoming call. This one from Chuck.

'I gotta go.'

'Good luck, honey. I love you.'

'Love you, too, Mom.'

He answered Chuck's call. 'Chuck? Sorry, my friend, but I got to run. Can I call you back later?'

'Er…sure. Just thought I'd let you know that Charlie rang me.'

He stilled. 'She did?'

'Yeah. She wants me to fly her to the airport. Her and Alice. I'm meeting her at the bay in an hour. She leaving already?'

'I hope not. Listen, I've got to rearrange a few things here, as I've got patients in the clinic, but can you do me a favour?'

'Sure.'

'Stall her?'

'Charlie?'

'Yeah. I need to see her before she goes. I mucked up, I need to apologise and I'm hoping to persuade her to stay.'

'Okay. Can do. I must say we all think you'd make a great couple.'

'We *all*? Who's *we all*?'

'Vasquez.'

'What?'

'Talk of the town, mate. You think patients and staff haven't noticed the way you two look at one another? You think you're hiding it, but when you ride through town in the back of a truck cradling her after a fall, people begin to talk.'

'Okay, okay. I get the picture. But you can stall, right?'

'Sure. I can tell her the right rotavator needs cranking.'

'Do planes have rotavators?'

'Does it matter?' He could hear Chuck's smile in his voice.

'No. I guess it doesn't.'

CHAPTER SEVENTEEN

'WHAT'S TAKING SO LONG, Chuck?' Charlie kept glancing at her watch as she sat in her wheelchair on the small wooden pier.

The pilot had opened a flap to expose part of the plane's engine. It all looked terribly complicated inside.

'Just some final checks. You wouldn't want us to fly without me checking it's safe for you and this precious cargo, huh?' he said, ruffling a sulky Alice's hair.

'No. Of course not.' She checked her watch and looked out behind her. She didn't think Eli would come chasing after her. Not after the way they'd parted. Not after the resignation letter she'd left on the clinic desk. Had he seen it yet? He might not have. Especially if he didn't have any clinic patients yet. She'd wanted to leave it in his office, but the door had been locked and, quite frankly? She'd wanted to get out of there, the sooner the better. Especially in this damn chair.

Nothing had gone right for her since coming here and now she was flying back to what? Home? That was a joke. She didn't really have one. The only place she'd ever felt comfortable living in had been here, strangely. Was that personal growth? Or just because Alice had begun to settle in a place? She'd certainly grown attached to Mrs Clark and Eli…

But so had she.

And that was why she had to go. Because how could she allow herself to get attached to someone who wasn't prepared to get attached to her? He'd only wanted a fling anyway, so this was no biggie, right? And she was sick of making mistakes over men.

'Can't we at least get in the plane? It's chilly out here on the pier,' she complained to Chuck.

'Sorry. Aviation rules. Pre-flight checks have to be completed first.'

She had no idea if that was true, but Chuck didn't look sorry. Not one bit. In fact, he looked a little amused, if anything.

Behind her, she heard footsteps clomping towards her on the wooden pier. Then they stopped. She knew whose footsteps they were and felt her heart sink.

'Charlie?'

It was him.

'Eli!' Alice dropped her rucksack and went running towards him and, as before, he scooped her up high into the air.

'Hey, pumpkin.'

She watched as Eli kissed her daughter on the head and gave her a huge squeeze.

Chuck closed the engine flap, wiped his hands on a dirty rag and gave her a smile as he passed. 'Hey, Alice. Come and look at these geese with me. Leave your mom and Eli to talk in private.'

And that was when she realised that Chuck had been stalling intentionally. Long enough for Eli to get here.

She stared at Eli. 'You made him stall us?'

'Guilty as charged, Your Honour.'

'Why are you here, Eli? There's nothing more to be said. You've made that abundantly clear.'

'You're wrong. There's plenty to be said.'

'Like what? Enlighten me, why don't you?'

He took a few more steps towards her. 'Not here. On the pier, it's exposed. Can we go over there and talk?' He pointed at a waterside bench.

He wore jeans, a fitted tee and a loose flannel shirt over the top. Rugged work boots on his feet made him look like a grungy rock star, rather than a doctor who had just come from a clinic. But that was Vasquez for you. It was more relaxed out here. It was why she liked it. As he settled onto the bench, he took a deep breath.

'I was wrong before. To not tell you what you wanted to hear.' He sighed. 'I was being stupid.'

'You won't hear me arguing.'

'Will I hear you be quiet, so I can say what you want me to say?' he asked with a smile.

She opened her mouth to respond, thought better of it and clamped it shut again.

'Thank you. Charlie…of course I want you to stay. You and Alice. And if not for me, then for that little girl, who loves it here and wants to stay.'

'You want me to stay?'

'Of course I do!'

'Why? Tell me why, exactly, you want me here.'

'Because…you have never been out of my mind, Charlie Griffin. I had to leave you once and I hated it and when you walked back into my life again, I couldn't believe my luck. But I didn't think you'd want to stay for me, because I can't give you what I know that you want.'

'And what do I want?' she asked breathlessly.

'You want a family. You want loads of kids. You said so, only recently.'

'And you think I want that with you?'

'Don't you?'

Now it was her turn to look uncomfortable. 'I'd be a liar if I said I hadn't thought about it.'

'I can't give you kids, Charlie. I'm sterile. I had testicular cancer in medical school and we found out then. The Clarks? They got me through the worst time in my life. A time in which I was scared. Surgery. Chemo. They kept me strong. Mom sitting by my bedside every day. Dad getting me out in the fresh air when I had the energy. Like I was their actual, biological child. They wept for my pain. Would have suffered for me in my place if they could. I couldn't have got through it without them and that was when I realised I truly was one of them.'

Cancer? Her heart ached for him! What an awful thing for him to have gone through! And she'd thought his life had been perfect since he was adopted.

I was wrong.

'I thought if we kept it simple between us—a fling—then it would be easy to say goodbye. But it has never been easy to say goodbye to you and I don't want to have to do so again. I may have gained a family here, but I have also lost so much.'

'I can't stay here. There's no job for me.'

'There is. Nance has informed me that she doesn't want to return full-time after her maternity leave is over. She even said she might not return ever. So there is a post for you. A job share, at least.'

'Why should I stay?'

'Because you love it here. Because Alice loves it here. Because the people here love you and I…' He took her hands in his. 'Because *I* love you.'

It was all so much! He'd gone from telling her nothing to telling her everything and it was all so overwhelming!

'I don't know what to say.'

'If you don't love me back, then say goodbye and do it quickly, because I don't think I could do another long, drawn-out goodbye. But if you feel the same way as me…then stay. We could build a life together. A great life. You, me, Alice.'

'We could adopt,' she said, the words surprising her as they came out of her mouth.

'What?'

'We could do what your mom did. Adopt a kid who needs a home. Maybe more than one, if we wanted. We could build a family that way. We're ideally situated to understand what that gift would mean to a child. What do you think?'

He smiled. Broadly. And she felt her heart lift.

'I would do anything to make you happy.'

She smiled back, felt tears of happiness pricking at her eyes. Wanted nothing more than to stand and wrap her arms around him and pull him close, but she couldn't.

'You make me happy,' she said. 'You're enough. You've always been enough.'

'I love you, Charlie Griffin.'

'And I love you, Eli Clark.'

And he reached for her, cradling her face in his hands as he gave her a long, deep kiss.

EPILOGUE

'I'M NERVOUS!'

Eli pulled her close. One to stop her from pacing, but two…he just liked having her close and looking into her eyes. She softened when he did so. The frantic worry would leave her face and she would relax. 'Take a breath. Look at me. We're gonna do great.'

'How can you know for sure? We've never done this.'

He smiled. 'I know what it's like to be chosen and to drive off in a car with a couple you've only met a couple of times.'

'Do I look okay? Do I look like a good mom?' she asked, glancing down at her outfit. A beautiful soft blue summer dress, dotted with white daisies.

'You look perfect.'

'What about me? I'm about to be a big sister,' said Alice.

They both turned to her. She'd been so thrilled about the idea of having a sibling and she'd wanted to choose a gift to give to David. Picking out a dump truck and a football and a colouring book with a pack of felt-tip pens to go along with it.

'You look great,' Eli said. He liked that he could help reassure and calm them down, because honestly…? He was pretty nervous himself. This had been a long time coming. A lengthy process they'd gone through to be able to go to an orphanage and choose a child with the help of the agency they were doing it through. There'd been many sets of paperwork. Lots of background checks. Plenty of visits. And they'd finally settled on David. A little boy, three years of age, who had been abandoned at a fire station when he was six weeks old.

As orphans, both he and Charlie were in the special position of knowing the gift they were giving to a child and to each other in building their family.

He'd never known a proper home, but he and Charlie had fallen for David's cheeky smile and lively character from day one. He had a great chuckle. It was infectious! And at their last visit, he'd fallen asleep on Charlie's lap for over an hour, snuggled into her and she'd looked so beautiful, sitting there, stroking the little boy's golden hair.

How could it possibly have been anyone else?

And here they were today. Ready to take him home to Vasquez.

It had been a kind of whirlwind, the last year and a half. Charlie had gone permanently full-time at the clinic—though she was going on maternity leave once they got home with David—Alice had had a piece of art win a competition on a children's show on TV and they'd moved into a bigger home. One that would be big enough for the family they aspired to build.

He had adopted Alice officially.

The door opened and in walked Karen, the support worker they'd been working with, and standing beside her, holding her hand, was David. He beamed when he saw them and ran forward into Charlie's arms.

She scooped him up and hoisted him onto her waist. 'Hey, you!'

'Hi,' he said.

'I have a question for you.'

'Okay.'

'Do you want to come home with us?'

He nodded, smiling. 'To stay?'

'Yes. For ever and ever.'

'For ever and ever?' he repeated, his eyes lighting up.

'That's right,' Eli said.

'Yay!'

Eli scooped up Alice and moved closer so that Alice and David could hug. They'd both got on so brilliantly with each other from day one. 'Let's go home.'

They waved goodbye to Karen after she'd walked them to the truck with David's case of clothes and a couple of teddy bears he liked.

As they drove away, with their two kids chattering in the back of the truck, Charlie reached for his hand and squeezed it. 'We did it.'

He raised her hand in his and kissed it. 'We did. I love you.'

She smiled at him, quickly glancing at the two kids in the back seat—the start of their big family.

'I love you, too.'

* * * * *

If you enjoyed this story, check out these other great reads from Louisa Heaton

Bound by Their Pregnancy Surprise
Snowed In with the Children's Doctor
The Brooding Doc and the Single Mom
Second Chance for the Village Nurse

All available now!